TALES OF THE DARK FOREST

KNYGHTMARE!

STEVE BARLOW & STEVE SKIDMORE

ILLUSTRATED BY FIONA LAND

HarperCollins *Children's Books*

First published in Great Britain by HarperCollins *Children's Books* in 2004
HarperCollins *Children's Books* is a division of HarperCollins*Publishers* Ltd,
77-85 Fulham Palace Road, Hammersmith, London, W6 8JB

www.harpercollinschildrensbooks.co.uk

2

Text copyright © Steve Barlow and Steve Skidmore 2004
Illustrations by Fiona Land 2004

ISBN 0 00 710866 4

The authors and illustrator assert the moral right to
be identified as the authors and illustrator of the work.

Printed and bound in England by Clays Ltd, St Ives plc

TALES OF THE DARK FOREST

KNYGHTMARE!

Find out more at:
     www.the2steves.net

The Legend of the Dark Forest

According to legend, the Dark Forest was not always dark. Long ago, the Kings of the Forest ruled a rich and fertile land from their high throne in the great City of Dun Indewood. Their prosperous and peaceful realm was defended by brave and honourable Knyghts, and you couldn't throw a rock without hitting a beautiful maiden, a sturdy forester or a rosy, apple-cheeked farmer. (Of course, none of the contented citizens of Dun Indewood would ever dream of throwing rocks about anyway; and if they did, one of the Knyghts, who were not only brave and honourable but just and kindly, too, would ask them very politely not to do it again.)

It was a Golden Age.

But over the years, the Knyghts and Lords of the City grew greedy, idle and dishonest, and fell to quarrelling among themselves. The line of the Kings died out.

The power of Dun Indewood declined. Contact with the other cities and towns that lay in the vast wilderness of the Dark Forest became rare, and then was lost altogether when the Forest roads became too dangerous to travel.

The creatures of the Forest became wild and dangerous until only a few hardy souls dared to brave its perils. The citizens of Dun Indewood continued to argue among themselves and cheat each other, turning their backs on everything that happened outside the City walls.

With no one to tame it, the Forest became home to truly dreadful things. Beasts with the understanding of men, and men with the ferocity of beasts, roamed the dark paths. The trees themselves became malevolent and watchful. And the Forest grew...

Well, that's the legend, anyway.

Of course, these days, nobody believes a word of it...

Ye Mappe of
Ye Darke
Foreste
(as it hath thus
far been
discoverede...)

Mount Inside

Here be Trolls

Castle
Wideawake
(formerly the Sleeping Castle)

Rose's
Cottage

The
Forest
River

The Ragged Mountain

Grandmama's
House

Great West

Jenny Greenteeth's Pool

Dragons of the
Darke Foreste

Hills and Pinewoods

Here be Dragons

CHAPTER ONE

H ow the Story Began and our Heroes came to a Sticky End.

"Did you hear that?"

Without waiting for a reply, Will threw off the cloak that had covered him as he slept and rose into a crouch. Ears straining for any sounds of danger, he looked around.

Night lay heavily over the Dark Forest. There was no wind: not a ripple disturbed the lake beside which Will and Rose had made their camp. The light of the new moon barely penetrated the thick canopy of leaves overhead; only in the water was it reflected as a glimmering bar of silver across the dull, smooth surface. The campfire had burnt down to embers, which cast a faint red glow across the clearing.

On the other side of the fire, Rose's sleeping roll lay crumpled and empty. Turning his back on it, Will reached down with his left hand to loosen the bindings of his sword. Gripping the hilt, he began to inch the blade from its sheath. Wrapping his cloak round his left arm as a makeshift shield, he peered intently into the shadows between the trees.

There was movement to his left, a whisper of cloth, and a girl of his own age appeared at his side. Rose's piercing blue eyes narrowed as she peered into the darkness of the Forest, crossbow at the ready. "Did you hear a noise?"

"Yes," said Will.

"So did I." Gazing intently into the surrounding darkness, Rose jerked her head. "It came from over there."

Will said carefully, "Then I think we may be in trouble."

"Why?"

Will pointed his sword towards the opposite side of the clearing. "Because the noise I heard came from over *there*."

"You mean we're surrounded?"

"It looks that way," said Will. "The question is, what by?"

"By what!" The new voice – loud, harsh and disgruntled – came from a dusty bag lying at Will's feet. "'What by?' is ungrammatical."

Will gritted his teeth. "This isn't the time for a language lesson."

"Oh, we're talking about time now?" said the voice in sneering tones. "Well, as you brought it up, I have something to say about time. The time, by my estimation, is currently quarter past sleepy-byes, so just exactly why are you two running about screaming the place down in the middle of the night while some of us are trying to get a little rest around here, thank you so much? Would you mind explaining that?"

Rose kicked at the bag, which went, "Ouch!"

"Shut up," she hissed. "Something's out there."

"Something's out there?" The voice rose to a near-hysterical pitch. "Of *course* there's something out there! This is the Dark Forest. We've been traipsing through it for months, ever since we left Dun Indewood with it's warm beds and regular meals – wasn't *that* a great idea! You know very well that there's *always* something out there! Now will you please go kill it, or let it kill you? I don't much care which as long as you're *quiet* about it!"

Will stabbed his sword point-first into the ground and tugged at the bag's drawstrings. It opened and he pulled out a magnificent wooden harp, the frame of which was topped with a crowned head. The carved face scowled up at Will. "So now you drag me out of bed," the Harp said wearily. "What is your problem?"

"Our problem," Will answered, "is that we're expecting to be attacked at any minute."

"Well, what am I supposed to do about it? Sing them into a coma?"

Out of the corner of her mouth, Rose said, "It wouldn't be the first time."

"Oh, har-de-har. Suddenly everyone's a comedian."

Will shook his head. "Nobody expects you to fight. But

you can watch and warn us if anything comes." He leaned the Harp against his pack, facing out across the clearing, then retrieved his sword. Silently, he and Rose moved to the water's edge so that their flank was protected by the lake while they and the Harp had a clear view in all directions of the grim, gnarled trees that surrounded them.

After a few moments the Harp hissed, "Hey! Are you two watching my back?" Will and Rose, intent on their vigil, made no reply. "I said, are you watching my back?" The Harp's strings began to rattle. "It's all very well for you humans," it whined. "You can turn round on account of having legs. I can only see from side to side, I'm feeling very exposed here... *What was that?*" The Harp's voice rose in a shriek of dismay. "I saw something! There *is* something behind me! It's got an axe! A big axe! A big sharp axe! It's creeping up on me! I can hear it! Do something!"

Rose gasped. "You're right! There is something terrible behind you."

The Harp shuddered. "What is it?"

"Me! And if I hear another peep out of you, you're matchwood!"

Rolling its eyes, the Harp subsided.

For several more tense minutes, Rose and Will scanned the surrounding darkness, every sense straining to catch any sound or movement that would indicate the presence of hidden watchers. At length, Rose removed the bolt from her crossbow and returned it to the quiver at her waist. She gave Will a slightly shamefaced grin. "I suppose we must have been hearing things."

Will remained watchful. "I don't think so."

"Then it must have been an owl or something."

"What I heard was no owl."

"Oh, please yourself." Rose yawned. "I'll put some more wood on the fire." She picked up the Harp.

"Hey!"

"Only joking." Rose put the Harp down and picked up a dead branch. "This time," she added under her breath.

"Funny lady," the Harp muttered in sour tones. "You crack me up."

"Don't tempt me." Casually, Rose broke the branch across her knee and tossed it on to the fire.

With a whoosh, flames shot up as though the wood had been soaked in oil. With a startled cry, Rose stepped back, Will stared frantically from side to side – and with a terrifying howl that sent leaves tumbling from the trees, their enemies were upon them.

A squadron of dragons swooped overhead, flaming. Will-o-the-wisps swarmed from the trees. Amid the unearthly flickering light and the bursts of dragonfire, the denizens of the Dark Forest hurled themselves upon Rose and Will.

An army of terrible creatures poured out of the shadows. At its head charged a cavalry regiment of spriggans; uncouth, goblin-like creatures clad in skins and wielding stone hammers and axes. They were mounted on aughiskies; enormous demonic horses with flashing hooves and flaming red eyes. Charging with them were packs of ferocious hell-hounds; barguests and padfoots, baying for blood. Behind them came the infantry; platoons of shrieking goblin-like hobyahs and henkies. Among them strode the giants; one eyed fachans, bounding along on their single legs, and jabbering firbolgs, swinging clubs made from whole trees.

"They're coming! They're coming!" shrieked the Harp unhelpfully. "Save me! Women and plucked-string instruments first! What am I saying? Forget the women!" It stared in wide-eyed terror at the legion of approaching leprechauns, brandishing brass-bound shillelaghs.

The first wave struck. Will ducked to avoid the clutching hands of a nucklavee and slashed at the giant, skinless centaur with his sword. At his back, Rose shot bolt after bolt into the screaming horde with no visible effect. Will dispatched a firbolg, then had to dive out of the way of a gigantic cudgel-wielding Jack-in-irons, the heads of its former victims swaying horribly at its waist.

"Let's lighten up, people! Whatever your beef is, I'm sure if we just sit down and discuss this, we can reach some kind of negotiated settlement. Violence never solved anything – put that axe down! Aaaa...!" The Harp's panic-stricken pleas ended in a horrible sound of crunching, twanging and splintering wood.

Will looked round just in time to see Rose stagger under the attack of a suicide squad of redcaps. A split second later she disappeared beneath a cackling tide of the fearsome creatures, all tearing off their gruesome headgear in unspeakable delight at the prospect of re-dyeing it in human blood. With a howl of rage, Will sprang to her aid, but a savage blow from a spriggan's axe sent his sword spinning out of his hand. Then he was dragged down by his leering enemies and held as the final horror appeared: the indescribable, shapeless monstrosity that was Boneless, wallowing unspeakably towards him. It reared up and fell clammily forwards to engulf him in its abominable, soul-destroying embrace, as...

Will screamed himself awake.

It was morning. The fire had gone out and a faint mist was rising from the lake to wreathe the trees in questing fingers of vapour. On the other side of the fire, Rose was sitting bolt upright, shivering and staring wide-eyed at nothing. Gasping for breath, Will said, "Are you all right?"

Rose gave a shudder and nodded.

"Bad dream?"

Rose drew her knees up to her chest and clasped her arms around them. In a strained voice, she said, "Horrible. You were being eaten alive by gobblings."

"Oh?" Will felt strangely miffed that Rose should dream such an inglorious end for him. "I didn't fight them off?"

"There were too many."

"And what were you doing while this was happening?"

"I'd been captured by a dreadful ogre. I couldn't get to you. It was horrible. You were screaming and screaming..."

"Oh, I was, was I?"

"Oh, yes – and the gobblings were drooling all down their bibs and stabbing you with their forks and carving lumps off you with their knives and dipping their spoons into—"

"Yes, thank you, you don't have to draw me a picture." Will wiped cold sweat from his brow.

"You can draw *me* a picture." The Harp's voice was muffled by its bag. "With all the gory details. Does liver come into this? Or entrails? Tell me the whole offal truth!"

Will dragged the Harp from its bag. "The last time I saw *you*," he told it acidly, "you were being smashed to smithereens by a bunch of giants."

"Really?" the Harp gulped. "Why?"

"Maybe they were music lovers," said Rose.

The Harp pouted. "You know, lady, it's too bad I don't dream, because I could really enjoy a nice vivid nightmare where you get turned into kebabs. You catch my drift?"

Will rose stiffly to his feet and stretched. "This has been happening a lot lately. Bad dreams, I mean."

Rose nodded. "Ever since we passed through that wall of mist a couple of days ago. I said at the time there was something uncanny about that."

Will couldn't actually remember Rose saying this, but it didn't seem a good moment to question the accuracy of her memory. "Maybe somebody – or something – is trying to warn us."

"Warn us about what?"

Will shrugged.

"There doesn't seem much point in warning us, unless whoever is doing the warning tells us what it's warning us about," complained Rose, busying herself with the fire. "But there must be something strange going on. I don't usually get bad dreams."

Will dug out a badly dented cooking pot from his pack

and dipped it into the lake. "Me neither. Mostly, the dreams I remember are good ones."

"Are they?" The terror had left Rose's face to be replaced with a look of mischief. "Such as what?"

Will felt his cheeks go red. "Well, sometimes I dream that I'm a Knyght... in shining armour, you know." Will tapped ruefully at his battered breastplate. A flake of rust fell off. "And I'm rescuing a maiden..."

Rose gave him a narrow-eyed look. "Is that so?" she snapped. "A poor, simpering, helpless maiden I suppose, with masses of blonde hair and lips like rosebuds. And why is it always *maidens* that need rescuing, I wonder? I seem to recall rescuing *you* on quite a few occasions!"

Will said nothing, mostly because this was true. Rose had spent her whole life in the Forest and knew far more about its pitfalls than Will, who had been brought up in the relatively safe shadow of Dun Indewood's walls. In the months following their departure from the City to explore the world outside, her Forest savvy had saved his hide more times than he cared to remember. "And don't you dare tell me," Rose went on, eyes flashing, "that sometimes the helpless maiden who needs rescuing in your dreams happens to look like me."

Will made a great show of being very busy about finding exactly the right spot in the fire to set the pot so that it would boil quickly and not fall over. Admitting that he had ever thought of Rose as a 'helpless maiden' was clearly not a sound survival strategy.

The Harp cackled. "Sap!" Then gave Rose a sly look. "So what about your dreams, toots?"

"Don't call me 'toots'!"

"C'mon," wheedled the Harp. "What happens in your dreams?"

"I don't have dreams," said Rose primly.

"You're human," said the Harp. "Of course you do."

Rose suddenly looked bashful. This was so unusual that Will's jaw dropped. "You'll think it's silly."

"Me?" The Harp sounded shocked. "Never! C'mon. Don't be shy. Tell Uncle Harpie."

"Weeell..." A faraway look came into Rose's eyes. She looked down at her travel-stained homespun skirt and tunic. "Sometimes," she said wistfully, plucking at a frayed edge of the coarse material, "sometimes I dream about being a princess, and having hair that shines, and wearing a beautiful white gown that floats around me like a cloud..." She gave Will a strange, shy, apprehensive look.

Will stared expressionlessly at Rose for several seconds, taking in the weaponry, the tanned, smudged face and the unkempt, twiggy plaits of dark hair. He shook his head. "No. Sorry. Can't see that."

"Me neither," agreed the Harp.

Rose gave them a furious glare. "Men!" She stamped her foot, turned her back on them and gazed out over the lake, her back rigid with disapproval.

Will belatedly realised that he probably hadn't been very tactful. "Sorry, I didn't mean—" He stopped. Something was happening in the lake.

The waters parted. From the lake rose an arm, clad in a sleeve of white silk interwoven with gold. In its pale hand, a magnificent sword glinted in the sun. Will gaped. It was just like an illustration from one of the books of Knyghtly valour he had read so long ago, at Knyght School in Dun Indewood. The Damsel of the Lake, a beautiful sword... Hesitantly, he reached towards it...

...and drew his hand back. A sword such as this wasn't for the likes of him. How could he, Will the poor swineherd, claim such a weapon? Even Squire Willum de Sanglier (the aristocratic name he had adopted at Knyght School) had no right to a blade like this. Surely this sword was meant to be found by some King or great warrior... and yet, what if it was meant for Will? Could he refuse such an adventure?

As he hesitated, there was a frantic splashing in the lake at his feet – and Rose sat up, still holding the sword, looking very wet and cross and spluttering for breath.

"For pity's sake make your mind up!" she complained. "I'm catching my death down here!"

Will stared. "Just a minute," he gulped. "If you're down there, who's next to me up here?"

He turned – and screamed as he came face to face with a foul hag. Cackling horribly, she lunged at him with fingers like talons. The Rose in the lake at his feet leapt up like an avenging fury, her skin creasing and changing. A forked tongue shot from her dry, scaly mouth, and snake eyes flashed implacable malice.

The water boiled as dozens of frightful merrows and dinny mara thrashed it with their powerful fish tails, and water-leapers rocketed from the depths with a great clatter of leathery wings, frog-like mouths gaping. Will tried to break away from the deadly lake and found himself wading into a vast host of demons. Bug-bears, hobgoblins, kitty-witches, efreets, changelings, hodge-pochers, wraiths, madcaps, boggleboes, hobbits, lubberkins, clappernappers, frittenings, lubberfiends and hundreds of other nightmarish Forest creatures swept over him, shrieking and giggling, in a living tide.

As the terrible creatures engulfed him, Will saw, on the far side of the clearing, the motionless figure of a gigantic Knyght on a great horse. The horse's coat and harness, the Knyght's armour and weapons – all were black as a tar pit. He appeared to be watching, intently but dispassionately, as the swarming horrors dragged Will down into a dreadful world of fear, pain and hopeless oblivion.

CHAPTER TWO

H ow the Whizzard was given the Run-around, and the Harp gave Will and Rose a Reality Check.

I n another part of the Dark Forest, Tym the Whizzard was mooching along faster than the eye could see, with his hands in his pockets. He was in a bad mood.

"Stupid sun," he muttered as its first rays shone through the leaves that hung motionless overhead. He squinted. "Stupid leaves." He ducked beneath a wood pigeon that hovered over the path, frozen in mid-wingbeat ("Stupid bird"), swayed to the left to avoid a squirrel caught in mid-leap ("Stupid squirrel"), and kicked savagely at a toadstool ("Stupid toadstool").

Not that anyone could hear Tym's complaints and sympathise. In fact, that was part of the problem. Tym was the Dark Forest's only Whizzard. Thanks to the potion he had first brewed as a young apprentice in Master Herbit's workshop, Tym could move so fast that he was, to all intents and purposes, invisible. Nothing and nobody could see him when he moved at Whizzard speed. No other creature in the Forest had this ability (apart from the almost-mythical Cumhera, which wasn't a sociable beast; and Humfrey the Boggart's pack of wish hounds, which weren't allowed to go with Tym in case they disgraced themselves by widdling on other people's rugs or eating their slippers).

For this reason, Tym's long journeys as the City of Dun Indewood's Chief Messenger and Emissary were solitary ones. No one could match the pace of a Whizzard. He didn't run with the pack, because the pack couldn't keep up.

"I wouldn't mind so much," he had complained to Zamarind, the granddaughter and heir of Lord Robat FitzBadly, ruler of Dun Indewood, before leaving the city on his current mission, "if only I thought I was doing something really important."

"Oh, aren't you doing anything important?" Zamarind had replied in her most vague and infuriating manner. "I thought you said you were."

"Well, it *ought* to be important," Tym said hastily. "I mean, if it wasn't for me, we wouldn't be able to communicate with that city Will and Rose discovered last year..."

"Oh, did they?" Zamarind's voice was languid, but the look she gave Tym sent a chill down his spine. "I don't recall. I must have been doing something else at the time."

Tym winced. Zamarind was making a not-very-subtle reference to an incident in which he had figured largely, involving a bungled robbery and an infuriated cockatrice whose lethal stare had left Zamarind in an unbreakable trance and near to death. Tym wished she would let the matter drop. After all, it could have happened to anyone.

"You know what I mean," he said. "Now we know about the city of Dinas Ruined, we can start to trade and make the roads safer. We need to be able to send messages back and forth." He sighed. "I just wish the messages were more interesting. I mean, it's hundreds of leagues to Dinas Ruined, it takes me days to get there even at Whizzard speed. On my last trip, I lugged that message from your grandfather all those miles through the Forest, facing untold dangers and all that" (Zamarind yawned.) "and I gave it to their ruler, and do you know what it said? 'Fraternal greetings and felicitations to the Archduke of Dinas Ruined.' And when the Archduke read it, he wrote a reply for me to bring back, so I lugged that all the way back here, and Lord Robat opened it, and it said, 'Charmed, I'm sure'. At this rate I'll have worn my legs to stumps before they've got through the formalities."

Zamarind gave him a heavy-lidded look. "Was that the only message?"

"Well no, but the others all said things like, 'Can you spare any cabbages?' or 'In Luigi's recipe for Firebelly Pasta, is the quantity of chilli given in pinches or pecks?'"

"Oh." Zamarind tossed back her silky, raven-black hair.

"So that's what you get up to all those weeks away in the Dark Forest. Carrying silly messages for Grandpapa – just so you've got an excuse to stay away from me, I suppose."

Tym spluttered at this injustice. "Your grandfather *sends* me. I have to go. Anyway, you hardly ever want to see me even when I *am* here."

Zamarind gave Tym another icy look. "One has affairs of state."

Tym groaned inwardly. When Zamarind started to refer to herself as 'One', he knew he was in trouble. It meant she had decided to stand on her dignity and high-born position. From then on, matters deteriorated, and angry words were exchanged until Zamarind gathered up her giggling waiting-women and flounced off, leaving Tym seething with baffled resentment.

He was still seething as he trudged moodily along the Forest path, occasionally ducking under an overhanging branch ("Stupid branch"). His journey, which had begun badly, had been made worse by a forest fire forcing him to make a lengthy diversion south of his normal route. Tym was tired, fed up and behind schedule. He had dozed fitfully for much of the previous night. Eventually, in the grey half-light before daybreak, he had given up even trying to sleep and set off to walk – at Whizzard speed, as there hadn't been enough light to move safely at wind speed, the intermediate running speed he usually adopted on his missions. From Tym's point of view he had been tramping along for hours, even though in the normal world the sun had only just risen. Time for a rest.

Tym slowed to normal speed. The sounds of the Forest – birdsong, the wind in the leaves, the terror-stricken squeals of small furry creatures and the bloodcurdling grunts of the big hairy things chasing them – wafted through the trees. Tym sat with his back against a gnarled trunk and closed his eyes. Within moments, sleep overcame him...

...and he found himself on a vast, windswept plain, bare of feature, devoid of life. Not a single star shone in a sky that was as black as midnight in a coal cellar. But outlined against that sombre vista, a gigantic human form, a thing of darkness and shadows, reared up above the plain to dwarf the tiny figure at its feet.

The shadowy figure spoke. *"Well met, Whizzard."*

"Dreamwalker!" Tym scrambled to his feet and bowed low. *"It is a long time since I last saw you."* He said this with a trace of nervousness. Tym had almost failed the first quest the Dreamwalker had set for him. He had accomplished his mission in the end, and the Dreamwalker seemed to have forgiven him – but this was a creature of enormous power and Tym had no wish to give it further cause for offence.

The Dreamwalker nodded its great shadowy head. *"Yes. I have been – occupied."* Tym was puzzled. The Dreamwalker seemed distracted, uncertain – almost worried.

After a pause, the Dreamwalker said, *"I trust that contact between your human cities is bearing fruit?"*

Vegetables actually, and cabbages to be precise, thought Tym, but aloud, he said, *"Yes."*

"*Good. It was for that purpose that I once called you to my world and gave you the abilities you now possess. I did so that you might help the scattered communities and peoples of the Forest to come together, so that they should have less fear of the Dark. But now, I need your help again.*"

Tym gulped.

"*When we first met,*" the Dreamwalker continued, "*I told you that the people of the Dark Forest had become afraid to dream, so that I was forced to withdraw and leave them prey to their fears. Yet one city – my own city, which above all habitations of men revered me and heeded my dreams – I never left. I have guided the people of that city, in their dreams, through all the dark years when the Forest grew and its people dwindled. But now...*" The Dreamwalker paused. A shudder seemed to pass through its great, insubstantial frame. "*Now, just as I begin to reach out to the minds of men elsewhere, I find I can no longer enter my own city. There is a barrier, which I cannot cross.*"

The Dreamwalker's deep voice was filled with anguish. "*I can no longer send dreams to my people. And without dreams...*"

Tym remembered the Dreamwalker's words on their first meeting. "*There are only nightmares,*" he said.

The Dreamwalker shook its great head. "*No. There is only... the Knyghtmare.*"

"It was a dream," soothed Rose. "A bad dream."

"It was horrible!" Will was trembling uncontrollably and he couldn't stop. "You turned into a... and then there were all the..." He yammered wordlessly for a while. "And lots of... things with teeth..."

"Tell me something I don't know!"

"I thought I was going mad."

"A few minutes more and you would have been. It's a good job I woke you up."

Will couldn't ignore this piece of historical inaccuracy. His trembling stopped instantly and he gave Rose a stony look. "I beg your pardon! I woke *you* up."

"You did not! I woke myself up."

Will spluttered helplessly. "You were in no state to wake anyone up!" he protested. "You were in a panic."

"You panicked!" Rose retorted hotly. "I didn't!"

"So why did you grab hold of me?"

"I didn't! You grabbed me!"

"Well, if you didn't grab hold of me, you can let me go now, can't you."

"You let go first."

Will did so. Rose stepped hastily back and jammed her hands tightly beneath her armpits in an effort to stop them shaking.

"So if you weren't in a panic," Will persisted, "how come you woke up screaming?"

"That wasn't screaming, that was a battle cry!" Lowering her voice, Rose added hesitantly, "I suppose... we are awake now?"

Will snorted. "Of course we are."

"How do you know?"

Now it was Will's turn to hesitate. "Well... I feel awake."

"Yes, but we felt awake last time, didn't we? I mean, we were just talking normally..."

"Arguing."

"Exactly, talking normally... about our dreams, and you told me about your dream of being a Knyght in shining armour, and I told you about..." Rose flushed. "About *my* dream, and then suddenly I was in the water..."

"Wait a minute!" Will's mind was racing. "What you're saying is, when we came out of the first nightmare and we thought we'd woken up, we hadn't really woken up at all; we were still dreaming, but we were dreaming we were awake?"

Rose's brow furrowed. "I suppose so."

"But all that you just said, about telling each other our dreams, I dreamed those things too."

"So?"

"So we were both having *exactly* the same dream." Will shook his head. "That's not normal, is it?"

Rose stared at him. "I have just been," she said emphatically, "torn limb from limb... twice... by the very nastiest creatures the Dark Forest can produce, and watched the same thing happening to you, and now you're talking about what's *normal*?"

Will tried again. "Yes, but... you have a bad dream, fair enough. I have a bad dream, fine. We both have a bad dream at the same time – getting weirder, but it could happen. But for us *both* to have the *same* bad dream...?"

Will shook his head. "That's not natural."

"You mean – somebody's doing something to us? Like a spell?"

"Maybe," said Will unhappily. "I don't know."

Rose sighed. "You could be right. But it doesn't make any difference. The point is, last time we thought we'd woken up, we were still dreaming, but we didn't know we were dreaming, we thought we were awake." A thought struck her. "Are we actually awake now?" She glanced around at their surroundings. Early morning mist drifted across the forest clearing and hovered over the silver-grey surface of the lake. "Where are we? In the dream world? Or..." She spread her hands helplessly.

"The waking world?" suggested Will.

"Yes, if you like. How will we know?"

"Woooaaaarrrrrrr!" They were interrupted by a muffled yawn.

Will stared at the triangular bag leaning against his pack. "The Harp's back in its bag."

"Well?"

"But I remember taking it out of the bag."

"You only dreamed you took it out of the bag."

"So if I take it out of the bag now, will I really be taking it out of the bag or only be dreaming I'm taking it out of the bag?"

Rose shrugged. "Suppose you try dreaming that you leave it in the bag."

"What will that prove?"

"Nothing. But it would be less annoying."

Will took the Harp out of its bag. It blinked around sleepily and smacked its lips. "Good morning, pilgrims. Did I miss anything?"

Rose rolled her eyes and Will explained their situation, while the Harp stretched its frame and tightened its strings.

The instrument gave a bark of laughter. "So you're telling me you don't know what's real and what isn't? Classic!" A sly look passed across its carved wooden face. "I can tell you whether you're awake or not."

Rose gave it a sceptical look. "All right. Tell us."

"How are you going to make it worth my while?"

"By not throwing you in this lake, which is what I'll do if you don't tell us," replied Rose, matter-of-factly.

The Harp was cowed. "No need to be so tetchy. OK, here it comes... You're awake!"

Rose folded her arms. "And how do you make that out?"

"Because I'm talking to you, right? And if you were dreaming, that would mean I'd have to be dreaming too. But..." The Harp played a crashing chord and announced triumphantly, *"I don't dream!"*

"Doesn't help," said Will flatly. "You don't have to be dreaming."

"But I'm talking to you!"

"No – we could be *dreaming* that you're talking to us. You might not be talking to us at all. You might not even be awake. It's happened before... twice."

The Harp boggled. "This is unbelievable."

"No," said Rose in a tight voice. *"That* is unbelievable." She pointed across the clearing.

An army came pouring out of the trees: a host of gibbering, misshapen creatures of all shapes and sizes – bogles, bugganes and bug-a-boos – swept into the clearing waving swords and axes, and screaming bloodthirsty battle cries.

"Here we go again," sighed Rose.

The Harp looked frantically from Will to Rose and back again. Will's sword was still fixed firmly in its sheath. Rose's crossbow remained undrawn. "What are you waiting for? You're going to fight them, right? I mean, that is your department, right? You're going to drive them off before they can do untold damage to, for instance, fragile, defenceless, highly inflammable Harps? Right?"

Will gave a resigned shrug. "What's the point? It's just another dream. They all end this way. We're going to get torn to pieces, whether we fight or not."

"If it's a dream!" the Harp pointed out frantically. "*If.* What if it's not? What if this is real?"

"It's not," said Rose flatly.

"You don't know that! You said so yourself. Just because this is how the other dreams ended, it doesn't prove *this* is a dream!"

"It doesn't prove that it isn't either!"

The Harp jangled frantically. "I don't *do* dreaming!" it screeched. "This is *real*, believe me!"

The hobgoblin horde was almost upon them. Will felt the first twinges of doubt. "I suppose it could be right..."

Rose shook her head stubbornly. "It's not real, Will."

An arrow flew out of the charging ranks, hitting Will's

breastplate with a clang. It snapped and spun away and Will stared at the bright mark its impact had made on the tarnished metal. "Well, that certainly *felt* real..."

"*Now* he admits it!" moaned the Harp, closing its eyes. "That was a real arrow, those are real ravening fiends and this is a real scream – aaaaaaaargh! Do something!"

An instant later, Will and Rose were standing back to back. The charging mob howled. Will's sword hummed and Rose's crossbow twanged as they faced the onslaught.

CHAPTER THREE

O f Dreaming Spires and Scheming Lyres
and Things that go Pop in the Fight.

"**B**ehold my city," intoned the Dreamwalker. *"Behold the dreaming spires of Beau Revere."*

In response to the Dreamwalker's sweeping gesture, a city appeared on the desolate plain. Tym gazed at it in astonishment.

There were indeed a lot of spires. The city of Beau Revere had more obelisks, towers, turrets, minarets, campaniles and other tall pointy things, than a hedgehog has prickles. They reminded Tym of a cake that Luigi the Pastafarian had produced for Zamarind's last birthday – a cake in the shape of a fairy-tale castle delicately crafted out of marzipan and icing (disappointingly presented on a foundation of lasagne). These buildings looked like that – as if nothing as solid and vulgar as brick or stone had anything to do with their construction. They were delicate. They were lofty. They seemed to reject the dull solidity of the earth and reach for the skies.

"*Very nice,*" said Tym, feeling that he should say something.

"*Come.*" The Dreamwalker pointed at the distant city. "*See!*" And suddenly, Tym found himself at the city entrance.

The gates were of bronze, and intricately worked with designs of constellations and astrological symbols picked out in precious stones. They swung apart and Tym passed through.

The city looked as if it had been built only yesterday. Everything gleamed. In Dun Indewood, Tym would have found himself walking on filthy straw, well mixed with the droppings of horses, cows, sheep, goats, pigs and geese – not to mention the unspeakable deposits inevitable in a city where public sanitation consisted of people emptying their chamber pots from an open window.

Nor was there any of the noise that was usual in Dun Indewood: there were no cries of traders and hucksters; no clatter of hammers; no clip-clop of hooves; no lowing, baa-ing and cackling from the beast market. Instead, there was simply the soft murmur of conversation, the distant ringing of a high-toned bell and the subdued rumble of a brightly painted cart pulled by soft-footed oxen.

And yet there were lots of people on the streets. Men

and women alike were dressed in jackets or tunics and loose trousers. The poor wore linen and went barefoot, but the rich wore silk and soft shoes with pointed toes. Some obviously wealthy men had sashes about their waists and strange padded hats that made them look as though they had cushions balanced on their heads. Their women wore small, delicately embroidered pillbox hats with gauzy veils which they sometimes used to cover their faces. The children were dressed like smaller versions of the adults. Greetings were courteous, conversations muted and polite. No one seemed to laugh, or shout, or sing... or play, or weep, Tym noticed, looking at the solemn-faced children.

It was the most serene place he had ever seen.

"This was my city," the Dreamwalker said in Tym's mind. *"Beau Revere, with its Dream Temples where citizens may go to dream undisturbed, or have their dreams interpreted by Dream Readers; Beau Revere, with its University of Dreams, where students sleep all the time."* (Tym wondered how this made them different from any other students, but he kept the thought to himself.) *"In my city,"* continued the Dreamwalker, *"men have never been afraid to dream, and they have always turned to me to shape their dreams. Here, my followers have interpreted those dreams, offering guidance and comfort. All through the decline of the Kings, the separation of the cities, the growth of the darkness, my people have dreamed."*

Tym thought, *"You say this was your city...?"*

"Indeed." The Dreamwalker seemed to sigh. *"Yet now, as the darkness over the world begins to lift, as the peoples of the Dark Forest begin to stir and reach out to one another; now that*

I begin to sense, once more, minds tormented by random, uncontrolled dreams, obscure, dark and meaningless; now, I say, my own city is closed to me." The Dreamwalker's voice was harsh, anguished. *"I show you Beau Revere as it was. I cannot show it to you as it is. I have no knowledge of what is happening there now. But I fear... I fear greatly!"*

With a savage cry, Will deflected a buggane's blade and turned his wrist to convert the parry into a powerful thrust that sent his sword right through his opponent's hairy body. On the instant, the creature's ugly, howling face dissolved into dust, along with the rest of it. Will stared at his sword stupidly.

"It," he croaked, "it just..."

"Went 'pop'. I know!" Rose was shooting from the hip as fast as she could draw her bow. All around her, bogles were coming apart at the seams as Rose's bolts pierced them through and through. "They're supernatural creatures. They shouldn't even be abroad in daylight. Will you snap out of it? I'm running out of ammunition!"

Will pulled himself together (something the bogles clearly couldn't do) and plunged into the fray. A bug-a-boo thrust its hideous face at Will with a dreadful cry of "Boo!". Will's backswing took its head off and it exploded into a cloud of dust that made him sneeze. Will shook his head unhappily. It wasn't exactly honourable combat when your opponents burst like balloons the instant you hit them.

Yet the bogles' weapons were real enough, as Will found out the hard way when a bug-a-boo's dagger sliced painfully into the flesh of his arm. Although the creatures themselves were vulnerable to a well-placed sword thrust, they held the advantage through sheer weight of numbers. The bogles and bugganes were savage fighters, and when one dissolved into dust, there were always three others to take its place. Rose had shot her last bolt, and had been forced to abandon her bow and draw her dagger. Will's parries became more and more desperate as his enemies pressed in. He found himself back-to-back with Rose, fighting for his life with fading hope.

"Try to force your way clear," he hissed to Rose. "I'll keep them busy while you get away..."

"Hah!" snapped Rose. "In your dreams..."

And suddenly, Will saw the black Knyght again – a dark shape wreathed in billowing clouds of white mist. Massive, immovable, unconcerned; observing with absolute detachment the struggle that was now nearing its inevitable and terrible end.

Then a coarse voice said, "Back off, ugly. Leave them to me."

There was a sudden pause in the fighting. A big, hard-faced buggane looked around menacingly and snapped, "Who said dat?"

"Boo!" said the first voice. "I did. What's it to you, gobbling-breath?"

"What did you call me?" The buggane lashed out

savagely at the bug-a-boo standing next to it. With a despairing, "Booooo!..." the hapless creature exploded. The other bug-a-boos muttered angrily.

"Tough guy," sneered a bogle voice. "Let's see you do that to someone your own size."

The buggane let out a roar and seized a terrified bogle, ignoring its cry of, "I never said nuffin'...!" A moment later, the bogle was a small cloud of dust.

"Hey, lads!" squeaked another bogle's voice. "Are we gonna let him get away with that?"

Shrieking with rage, the bogles turned on their erstwhile allies. Ignoring Will and Rose, who looked on in stunned silence, bogle fought buggane all over the field. Bug-a-boos fought both sides impartially and the battlefield rang with the clash of swords, shouts of "Boo!" and the sudden 'pop's as stricken fighters ceased to exist, sending up clouds of dust that blotted out the light.

And then, suddenly, the field was clear. A last buggane and bogle, striking out simultaneously, sent each other to a dusty end. When the cloud cleared, it revealed the Harp looking up at Will and Rose with a smirk on its face.

Rose stared at it. "Did you do that?"

The Harp nodded its head smugly. "Hey, look out, fellas!" it said in a squeaky bogle voice, "You've gone all to pieces!" It sniggered. "Ventrickorism – I learned it from a guy once," it went on in its own voice. "He was a tailor. Little feller, but clever. I heard he married a princess in the end, which just goes to show. And don't bother to thank me. Oh, you didn't."

Will wasn't listening. He stared across the dusty battlefield to where the Knyght in black had been. But there was no Knyght, no horse – just a few fading tendrils of mist sinking into the grass of the clearing, which was now beginning to ripple in a soft breeze that blew at the dust of their attackers, gradually spreading it far and wide.

"You're bleeding," said Rose disapprovingly. "I'd better bathe that. Come on." As she led him to the lake, Will kept glancing over his shoulder at the waving grass where their enemies had been.

"But why did they just turn to dust?" he demanded.

Rose tore a strip off Will's blanket and filled a cooking pot with water from the lake. "I told you," she said, rolling Will's sleeve up. "They're supernatural creatures." She scrubbed heartlessly at the wound on Will's arm.

"Ow!"

"Keep still. Anyone would think I was hurting you."

"You are!"

"Oh, don't be so wet." Rose rummaged in her pack, drew out a strip of fresh linen and wound it expertly round the cut. "There! Bogles and the others only usually come out at night," she explained, "and they form themselves out of dust – dust from under the bed or the top of the wardrobe... and in the morning they turn back into dust again. At least, they're supposed to. That's why it's a good idea to dust your house occasionally."

"But that lot didn't turn to dust when daylight came," Will pointed out, wincing. Rose's first aid was often more painful than the injury that made it necessary. He wondered whether she did it on purpose.

"No," said Rose thoughtfully, "they didn't. And that's worrying."

"Do you think the black Knyght set them on us?"

"What black Knyght?"

"The Knyght in black armour on a black horse—" Will broke off and stared at Rose. "You mean you didn't see him?"

"See who?"

"See whom?" snapped the Harp. Rose aimed a kick at it.

"Never mind." Will relapsed into silence, but his mind was racing. The black Knyght only appeared to me, he thought. Why? Was it some form of Knyghtly challenge?

Rose started to pack up their camp. "I'll tell you what," she said. "I bet whatever has been giving us bad dreams has something to do with what happened here."

Will nodded slowly. "And sometimes," he said, "you hear of dreams coming true."

Rose paused for a moment, and shivered. Then she fastened the straps on Will's pack and threw it at him with unnecessary force. "Coming?"

Grimacing, Will shouldered the pack, shoved the Harp into its travelling bag ("Hey!") and set off in Rose's footsteps.

The shadows beneath the endless trees of the Dark Forest rose up to meet them.

Tym stared apprehensively at the gigantic form of the Dreamwalker as the vision of the city faded around him. *"But why can't you go and see what is happening in Beau Revere?"*

The Dreamwalker clenched its giant fists. *"I am prevented! It is hard to explain – there is a barrier. I cannot see it, or feel it; but when I approach it, I find myself in a cloud of... darkness is not the right word, but I do not have a better one. And when I come out of the cloud, I find I am going in the opposite direction – away from the city, always away. The vision I have shown you – the shining city I remember – may by now be no more than a dream. I fear the worst."* The Dreamwalker seemed to shrink in size; its shadowy eyes with their sparkling depths seemed to bore into Tym. *"And I fear for the creatures like yourself who have gone there."*

"Like me?" Tym was thunderstruck. *"You mean humans?"*

"Yes. From your own City, I believe. A boy in battered armour who carries a sword and a harp, and a girl with a crossbow who fights like a warrior."

"Will!" cried Tym. *"And Rose! I met them once. It must be them."*

The Dreamwalker nodded its great head. *"So I feared, though I do not find it easy to tell one human from another unless they come into my realm."* Tym bit his lip. *"They went into the mist, where I could not follow."*

Tym was thinking furiously. *"Do you think they will get through the barrier? Will they reach Beau Revere."*

The Dreamwalker's voice was sombre. *"I cannot tell. But I fear for them. For I believe my city is now in thrall to another power, a new and dreadful power. And if your friends do reach it, they will be in danger. Terrible danger."*

Rose gazed at the city, shining in the clear early-morning light. "It's beautiful!"

Will wasn't so sure. From the hill on which they stood, the city stretched out on the plain below them had a fragile, ethereal air. Will's idea of a city was one with stone walls and battlements, stoutly built and easily defended. This city looked as if one well-thrown shot from a siege engine would cause it to shatter like a falling chandelier.

The Harp seemed to agree. At any rate, it eyed the city with disfavour, hummed a tinkly little tune in a sarcastic sort of way, and began to sing:

"When you wish upon a—"

"What?" Her reverie interrupted, Rose swung round on the Harp.

"Sorry," said the Harp sweetly. "It seemed appropriate, somehow." It gave the city another disparaging look. "What a dump. Can we go now?"

"No!" snapped Rose. "This is only the second city we've found – and the *only* one that looks..." Rose waved her hands about vaguely as she sought the right word.

"Twee?" hazarded Will.

"Like a cruet set?" suggested the Harp, innocently.

"Cultured!" snapped Rose. "Sophisticated! Refined! Elegant! All right?" The Harp snickered and Will stifled a chuckle. Rose stamped her foot and stormed off down the hill...

...Two hours later, they stepped through the great bronze gates, and into the streets of the city.

The echoing streets.

The deserted streets.

There was very little sound; but what there was, was disturbing. Muffled sobs. Distant shrieks. Wails and groans, which echoed from tower to lofty tower, as if the buildings themselves were crying out with pain.

"The further away we were, the better it looked." The Harp's voice was an apprehensive whine. "You know? What say we—?"

It broke off as a man rushed out of a side alley just ahead of them. He ran as if a pack of wolves were after him, uttering wild, unearthly shrieks. His eyes were wide and staring, and his mouth hung open like a wound. He was tugging at his hair, as if trying to tear it out a fistful at a time.

The figure didn't notice Will, Rose and the Harp until the last minute. He stopped short, staring at them as if he had suddenly found something worse than whatever was pursuing him. Then, with a scream that left all his earlier cries standing, the man turned and dashed back the way he had come.

Rose edged imperceptibly closer to Will. There was a

catch in her voice as she said, "What is *wrong* with this place?"

"You know, curiosity is a wonderful thing," yammered the Harp, "but not nearly as wonderful as self-preservation, so why don't we just turn right around, and—"

It broke off. A tall man with a gaunt face and a head as bald as an egg was now pacing down the deserted street towards them. His black silk robes, billowing with each stride, were covered from shoulder to hem in astrological symbols, picked out in silver.

As the figure passed, doors flew open and a tide of desperate-looking men and women flowed out on to the street. Their eyes were haggard, sunken, with shadows around them and bags beneath. They looked as if they had forgotten what sleep was – or perhaps, as if they were trying to forget. One or two of them kept brushing distractedly at their heads and shoulders, as if trying to dislodge malign things that no one else could see. They carried a menacing array of strangely curved swords, daggers, lances, scythes and axes.

The man in the black robes stopped in front of Will and Rose, staring at them with burning eyes. "Who are you?" he demanded. "What are you doing here?"

Will clenched his fists, but remembering he was a Knyght of Dun Indewood (or very nearly) said with polite formality, "I should be sorry to learn that your city has so far forgotten the courtesy due to guests and strangers..."

There were mutterings and bursts of bitter laughter from the mob.

"Strangers?" barked the man. "Guests? Spies and traitors, more likely! Witches and enchanters! Demons, perhaps!"

"Hey, now, look..." The Harp's voice was wheedling and conciliatory. "I'm sure we can work this out, whaddaya say?" A gasp ran around the crowd, followed by dark looks and darker mutterings. These people obviously weren't used to talking instruments and didn't much care for the idea.

Rose, without taking her eyes off the surrounding militia, gave the Harp a savage dig with her elbow. "Shut up."

The Harp ignored her. "Look, I can see you people are upset about something. You don't know us, you're worried, that's understandable... but let's just all calm down here, huh? Maybe you could direct us to an inn, or something, and we can sort all this out in the morning. I've always found, whatever the problem is, it'll all seem much better after a good night's sleep..."

With howls of rage and hate-filled eyes, the crowd pressed forward, weapons poised to strike. The robed man's eyes burnt even more fiercely and his ringing voice rose above the cries of the mob.

"Jinnees! Fiends! Creatures of the Knyghtmare!" Spittle flecked his lips. He pointed a quivering finger. "Seize them!"

CHAPTER FOUR

Of a Frightful Knyght, a Rude Vizier,
a Vague Emir and a Pest of a Jester.

Tym stared up at the Dreamwalker, open-mouthed with horror. *"I have to warn Will and Rose, before it's too late!"*

The Dreamwalker's dark eyes seemed to retreat further into shadow. *"I fear that the time for warnings has passed."*

"But they helped me on my quest," protested Tym. *"I have to find them – now!"*

Thinking of nothing but the urgency of his mission, Tym turned on his heel, and sped across the plain. The Dreamwalker made a sweeping gesture...

...and the sand of the plain shifted beneath Tym's feet, becoming soft, so that his feet slid back at every step. His legs became heavy, his feet leaden...

...and the shifting sands became mud, foul-smelling, clinging to his legs, slowing him further...

...and the mud deepened, until Tym was wading through it, waist deep, and the mud became thicker and thicker...

Tym stopped and hung his head. There was no way he could fight against the Dreamwalker in the creature's own realm and win. He said, *"Tell me what I must do."*

Instantly the mud vanished.

"There is a great evil at work," said the Dreamwalker. *"That evil is spreading. Who or what may be the cause, I cannot tell, but the answer must lie in Beau Revere."*

Tym clenched his fists in frustration. *"So you* do *want me to go there?"*

"All in good time," replied the Dreamwalker. *"Whizzard, I fear that this is too great a task for you alone – you will need the assistance of one skilled in penetrating the mists of confusion and falsehood."*

Tym thought for a while. Then he nodded slowly and a grim smile spread across his face. *"Like an inquestigator,"* he said. *"I know just the boggart."*

"Does this... boggart... possess the skills we need?"

"Well, he got me bang to rights." Ruefully, Tym cast his mind back to when Humfrey the Boggart, Dun Indewood's foremost (and only) private inquestigator, had discovered the secret of his Whizzard speed. *"He's the best there is."*

"Then you must seek this boggart's assistance and bring him to—" The Dreamwalker broke off with a startled cry. *"Is it even here?"*

Tym followed the Dreamwalker's gaze and gasped. A bank of fog was spreading out across the plain, its shimmering whiteness thrusting back the surrounding shadows. Leading the way, wraith-like wisps spread over the ground, gathering speed as they surged towards Tym and the Dreamwalker.

"This is a great power we face." There was anger in the Dreamwalker's voice: anger tempered by fear, and a kind of grudging respect. *"It dares to invade my kingdom..."*

Then the first tendrils of fog were upon them, curling themselves around Tym's legs like an arching cat demanding attention.

"Seek out the boggart and bring him to my world as soon as you can."

The fog was becoming thicker by the second, cutting Tym off from the Dreamwalker. The Whizzard peered into the vision-blurring greyness but could see nothing of the mighty creature. *"Dreamwalker!"* he called, but his cries were muffled by the fog. He could see nothing...

...and then, as swiftly as it had appeared and overwhelmed him, the fog thinned and receded.

Tym sat up, blinking at his surroundings. The Dreamwalker's world had disappeared. He was back on the Forest track, but fog still surrounded him on every side, blurring the shapes of the trees.

He staggered to his feet and gave a start as a roar of mocking laughter broke out from the depths of the fog.

"Hello!" Tym called out, nervously.

The laughter abruptly ceased, to be replaced by the

harsh neighing of a horse, then the steady drumming of echoing hoofbeats.

Derdum, derdum, derdum!

Tym looked around in panic, trying to get a fix on the sound. He tried to go to Whizzard speed and found to his dismay that something was preventing him. He felt confused, stupid, sluggish – almost incapable of movement.

Derdum, derdum, derdum!

The ground reverberated with the thudding impact of hooves. Tym stared helplessly into the fog. The drumming hoofbeats came nearer and nearer, louder and louder...

Derdum, derdum, derdum!

The monstrous shape of a Knyght, all in black and mounted on a pitch-black horse, erupted from the wall of white, its lance aimed directly at Tym's heart.

Tym screamed and screamed...

...and, like Will and Rose before him, awoke from the Knyghtmare.

Having been searched by the mob and stripped of their weapons, Rose and Will had been hustled through the deserted streets to a building that was, even by this city's standards, more than commonly ornate. Will correctly guessed this to be the palace. Here, they were turned over to a troop of guards with sharp, curved swords and haggard expressions. Still accompanied by their chief captor, the bald-headed man in black robes, they were marched through echoing corridors and at length hustled into an enormous room made up of tiers of arches, galleries and balconies. Marbled floors and walls were draped with silk tapestries and carpets. Eight pillars, chased with gold and as slim as wands, reached upwards to a huge circular domed roof, from which hung five silver chandeliers on delicately linked chains.

Alabaster urns stood in rows on golden plinths by the side of a pink marble channel through which ran a stream of bright turquoise water, cutting the room in two. Half a dozen large pink birds stood one-legged next to a bridge that spanned the water. The nearer side of the room was filled with men and women wearing expensive clothes and looks of near exhaustion. All were standing (some had to prop each other up) and many were trying, unsuccessfully, to smother yawns.

On the far side of the waterway was a raised dais on which stood a low throne covered in pearls and a host of precious jewels. A red silk cushion edged with gold braid perched on top of the throne, and upon it lay a small, tubby, vague-looking man in a bright blue turban. His puffy face was adorned with a tiny, pointed beard and curling moustaches that almost reached his ears. Servants stood beside the throne, wafting enormous white feathers over their master who appeared to be asleep.

Will felt the guards' hands pressing roughly on his shoulders, forcing him to his knees. At the same moment, their captor cried out in a ringing voice that raised echoes from every part of the room, "Bow, quail and quiver before His Most Phantasmagorical and Deluded Highness, King of Shadows, Visionary of Visionaries, Most Puissant Fantasist of the Intangible Dominions, Hereditary Grand Hallucinator, Emperor of the Chimerical and Dread Sovereign Lord of the Insubstantial Realm – Emir Raj, Lord of Beau Revere!"

The Dread Sovereign Lord of the Insubstantial Realm sat bolt upright and clutched at his turban, which had slipped down over his eyes. "What? What? By the sacred nightcap of my grandsires, Shaman, do you have to shout like that? I was just dropping off..." The Emir put a chubby hand to his cheek and his eyes widened in horror. "What am I saying? I nearly fell asleep, and if I had..." He gave a hollow groan. "Daughter!" he wailed. "Daughter! For shame! Your negligence is like to be my undoing!"

A black-haired girl, who until now had been lying curled at the foot of the Emir's throne, stretched like a cat and stared at Will and Rose with hooded eyes. Will was secretly amused to see Rose's hackles instantly rise. He could understand why. The girl was certainly very attractive – and, unlike Rose, as beautifully dressed, made-up and coiffured as art could devise.

She turned to the Emir, put her hands together palm to palm, and bowed gracefully. "A thousand pardons, O my father," she said in a husky voice that didn't sound at all apologetic. "Shall I call for your concubines, to beguile the hour with dance and sweet music?"

His Most Phantasmagorical and Deluded Highness gave a discontented wriggle. "Oh, don't bother," he said peevishly.

"To be honest, once you've seen one concubine, you've seen them all."

"Would my father see a miracle of rare device?"

"A stately pleasure dome with caves of ice?" The Emir snorted. "I've seen it. It's boring."

"Then, my father, shall I stay you with flagons and comfort you with apples?"

A look of panic crossed the Emir's face. "No flagons! No flagons! If I start drinking wine, I shall fall asleep, and if I fall asleep..." He shuddered.

The man in the black robes, who had clearly been waiting with increasing impatience to attract the Emir's attention, stepped forward. "Most Fanciful One," he cried in a ringing voice, "I have captured two spies from the unknown wastes beyond the city walls. Do you wish to interrogate them?"

The Emir gave Will and Rose a look of utter distaste. "Why in the name of all that's intangible should I want to do that? No. Bring me my jester."

The dark-haired girl looked thoroughly displeased. "But, my father..."

"I want my jester!" the Emir's voice rose to a petulant squeak. "Now!"

"Yes, my father." Tight-lipped, the girl rose and clapped her hands.

On the far side of the room, a bare-chested man struck a huge brass gong. The sound reverberated around the marbled galleries. The Harp, clasped to Will's chest, twanged discordantly as its strings hummed in sympathetic vibration. "Oohhh!" it moaned. "I hate it when that happens."

"Shut up," hissed Rose. "I don't think these people like talking instruments." The Harp gave her a mutinous look, but said nothing more.

As the reverberations subsided, a curtain parted on the far side of the room and a thin, anxious-looking young man bounded in. He was dressed differently from the courtiers. He wore a cap that fitted closely all round his head and tightly under his chin, leaving only his eyes, nose, cheeks and mouth visible. The cap had three floppy points, each with a bell on the end and, like his ill-fitting surcoat and tights, was quartered yellow and red. In one hand he held a stick topped by a wooden head that was the image of his own, and in the other, a string tied to the neck on an inflated bladder, which he flapped at the courtiers (to their evident annoyance). He hopped towards the Emir on the balls of his feet; left, right, left, right, his melancholy face changing as he stretched the sides of his mouth into a grin so wide that it looked as if it had been painted across his face. With his bent arms and legs, and fixed smile, he looked like a giant puppet, controlled by strings from above.

"Jester Scrape!" The Emir clapped his hands in delight. "Entertain us!"

Scrape shook his stick and waggled his head; the bells jangled. "Marry, good sir, riddle me this: what can fall on water, but never get wet?"

The Emir, an expectant grin on his chubby face, shook

his head. "No... no... ah, wait, I have it! Yes... no. No, you have me there."

"The answer..." the jester threw his arms out wide "...is a shadow." The Emir looked blank for a moment; then, as understanding dawned, he broke into peals of delighted giggles and clapped his fat little hands, while Scrape rang his bells and capered. All the other courtiers gazed at the leaping, parti-coloured figure with loathing.

The man in the black robes was by now almost beside himself with impatience. "Your pardon, Most Deluded Majesty, but we have no time for jests. There is serious business afoot."

The jester capered over the bridge and bounced his bladder off the black-robed man's bald head. "If your business is afoot, my lord Vizier, it must indeed stand. Yet a jest, too, is a serious business, for jesting is my business and by it I have my living." He jangled his bells in the Vizier's face, receiving a killing look in return.

The Emir cackled as if the jester had said something hysterically funny. "He has you, Vizier Shaman."

The Vizier directed a contemptuous look at Scrape, who was holding a silent conversation with the miniature head on his stick. From their sidelong glances and silent gales of laughter, it was clear they were mocking the Vizier. In a voice that dripped venom, the Vizier said, "I marvel that Your Abstractedness should find such antics funny."

"Ooops!" whispered the Harp. "Somebody's nose is out of joint." Will gave it a warning squeeze.

The Emir pouted. "You have no sense of humour, Shaman.

Come, Scrape, I am in the mood for fooling!"

The jester capered outlandishly. "Would my Lord hear a jest, a song, or a riddle?"

"A riddle!" commanded the Emir. "I love riddles."

"Then riddle me this, Sire: what has a neck but no head?"

The Vizier directed a burning stare at the jester and muttered (not quite loud enough for the Emir to hear), "You, if I had my way."

"Then I would surely be light-headed," Scrape murmured in reply. He shook his head until the bells jingled. "That is to say, light of my head."

The Emir, looking blank and expectant, cried, "Tell us the answer. What does have a neck, but no head?"

"The answer is – a bottle!"

"A bottle?" The Emir thought deeply for a moment before realisation dawned. "A bottle! Wonderful!" The Emir wiped tears of laughter from his eyes as Scrape hopped ludicrously around his throne.

The Harp groaned. "That guy needs to work on his act. He is one seriously lousy performer."

"Takes one to know one," hissed Rose.

The Harp gave her a haughty stare. "Your support and encouragement is totally underwhelming."

The Vizier shot the jester an acid look, then signalled to the guards. Will and Rose stumbled as their captors hustled them forward.

"Behold, the spies, most Deluded Majesty," he cried. "See how the vile wretches kneel and grovel before you in all their deficiency and unworthiness."

Rose pursed her lips and glared. The Harp muttered, "Charming."

Finally dragging his attention away from his jester, the Emir sighed. "Oh, very well, Vizier. You may question the accused."

"Accused!" Rose glared and sprang to her feet. "What are we accused of?"

There was a collective sharp intake of breath from the courtiers. The jester cuddled his head-on-a-stick, as though protecting it from this dangerous madwoman. The Emir's daughter, who had resumed her place at the foot of the throne, gave Rose an insolent and appraising stare.

The Vizier's voice rose to a near shriek. "Vermin! How dare you speak to His Most Phantasmagorical and Deluded Highness, King of Shadows, Visionary of Visionaries, Most Puissant Fantasist of the Intangible Dominions, Hereditary Grand Hallucinator, Emperor of the Chimerical and Dread Sovereign Lord of the Insubstantial Realm in such a rude fashion?"

"Exactly!" Clearly feeling that his dignity was threatened, the Emir shook his fists at Will and Rose. "You ask, what are you accused of? What are you accused of?!" He paused for a moment, then gave the Vizier a puzzled look. "What *are* they accused of exactly?"

The Vizier smiled condescendingly. "Your Whimsicality, they have entered the City of Beau Revere without express permission. They are evidently spies." The Vizier lowered his voice. "They may even know something about the disappearance of the Dreamwalker."

Will and Rose stared at their captor, then at each other. Tym had told them of the Dreamwalker. But according to Tym, the Dreamwalker was a giant, insubstantial creature who lived in his own dream realm, outside the world of the Dark Forest – how could it possibly have disappeared? And why was this important to the people of Beau Revere?

But the Vizier was still speaking. Pointing at the Harp, he declaimed, "Furthermore, they are evil jinnees and enchanters – they are in possession of a strange talking harp!"

The Harp's strings jangled. "A talking harp? What a ridiculous idea. The very thought of it! Who are you calling a talking harp?" There was silence as every eye in the room focused on the Harp, which closed its carved eyes. "Oops! There I go again! Me and my big mouth..." The Harp's eyes snapped open, and it rasped, "But I want it on the record that I'm not strange!"

"They're never going to believe that," muttered Rose.

Deciding on a diplomatic approach, Will remained on his knees. "Your... er... Vagueness, we have heard of this Dreamwalker, but we know nothing about your city, or what we're supposed to have done or anything—"

"Be silent!" The Emir stamped his foot. "All of you! I've never heard of such a thing. Who's in charge here?"

The Vizier bowed low, his gaunt face unreadable. "Why, you are, O Indefinite One."

"Exactly!" said the Emir snappishly. "Yet you come in here, interrupting my repose with spies and strangers and talking harps that make my poor head ache, even though you know I haven't slept for days and days..."

"None of us has, Majesty," said the Vizier tightly.

"Don't interrupt! None of you is to speak a word while I decide what to do with the prisoners." The Emir closed his eyes and his forehead wrinkled in thought. The silence went on and on. At length, the Emir opened his eyes again, and said in a sheepish voice, "What should I do with the prisoners, my daughter?"

"Burn them, O my father," said the dark-haired girl without hesitation. "Especially the female barbarian." Rose gave her a filthy look. Will stared at the Emir's daughter with great dislike, wondering how he had ever thought her beautiful.

"Capital idea!" The Emir beamed. "See to it, Vizier."

The Vizier was clearly holding on to his temper with difficulty. "O Questionable One, your wisdom and magnanimity is unsurpassed, yet there are those who would say that the prisoners should be tried before they are executed."

"Are there?"

"There are."

The Emir folded his arms. "Oh, well," he said pettishly. "If we must."

The Vizier turned to Will and Rose. "We shall soon discover the truth. As Chief Dream Reader of Beau Revere, I shall lay bare your innermost thoughts." He clapped his hands. "Bring in the dream viewer! Let the male prisoner come forward."

A servant entered with a red velvet cushion, upon which rested a glass sphere. The guards gestured Will forward. Handing the Harp to Rose, he approached the Vizier.

The Vizier took Will's wrist and pressed the palm of his right hand on to the sphere, while placing his own left hand on the smooth transparent surface. Rose watched anxiously. Will gave her what he hoped was a reassuring grin, but his heart was pounding. Then the Vizier lifted his right hand before Will's eyes, made a mysterious gesture...

...and Will fell instantly and deeply asleep.

So he did not see the circular dome high above them darken and fill with swirling cloud. He did not hear the gasps and screams of horror from the courtiers as the black Knyght on his black horse galloped through the parting mists, lance at the ready and pointing straight at the terrified Emir, who tried to hide under his cushion. All he knew was that when he awoke as instantly as he had gone to sleep, the courtiers were running around shrieking; Rose was calling his name and struggling frantically with the guards, and the Vizier, his face a mask of fear and hatred, was pointing a trembling finger at him.

"Fiend!" howled the Vizier. "Your dreams betray you! You bring the Knyghtmare to attack us even in the heart of our city. You will be tried in the Court of Dreams, and when you are found guilty...!"

The Harp strummed a funeral march. "Don't tell us," it sighed. "We'll be put to death – right?"

The Vizier's face was distorted by a truly dreadful grin. "Oh no," he grated. "Your fate will be more terrible than that. More terrible than you can possibly imagine."

CHAPTER FIVE

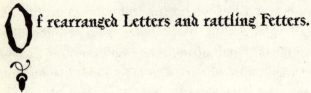

Of rearranged Letters and rattling Fetters.

Humfrey the Boggart stood at the foot of a rickety wooden ladder, looking upwards and scowling ferociously. Humfrey, who was about half the height of a man, thought human beings were ridiculously tall to begin with and disapproved of anything that made them taller.

The ladder was propped against a white building in the main square of Dun Indewood's fashionable district of Beau Monde. Clinging to its top and wobbling dangerously was the round figure of Luigi the Pastafarian. He was attaching the final letters on a gleaming sign above the entrance of his restaurant:

LUIGI'S TAPAS BAR

Humfrey snorted dismissively. "Not another name change!"

Startled, Luigi lost his footing and slipped several rungs down the ladder before his frantically clutching hands found a grip. The pastafarian glared down at Humfrey, his multicoloured dreadlocks quivering with indignation. "Mamma mia! You nearly make'a me fall!"

"Shay, I wouldn't do that if I was you," Humfrey advised. "And if you do, don't expect me to catch you. You'd shquash me flatter than a thin an' crishpy pizza."

Luigi grunted and descended the ladder, puffing hard. As he stepped back to survey the new sign, his frown disappeared and his habitual beam spread over his broad face. "What'a you think?"

"I think you're crazy!" Humfrey told him. "Last month, thish place was called *The Pizza Palace and Patissherie*, then you changed it to *Luigi's Pashta Bar*."

Luigi shrugged. "The patisserie wasn' doin' so good since Bertram stop makin' his rock cakes an' go back to Caer Borundum."

Humfrey gave a grudging nod. "Fair point – but now you're changing it again! I know guysh who don't change their netherdrawersh that often!"

Luigi gave him a pitying look. "Ma fren', you may be the best inquestigator in Dun Indewood, but you don' understan' the restaurant business." The pastafarian spread his arms wide. "To stay ahead, you gotta be innovative. You don' get nowheres by standin' still. You gotta move with the times! You gotta give the customers choice an' variety. You gotta be different."

Humfrey peered at Luigi's establishment with a jaundiced eye. "Sho what'sh 'tapash'?"

"Instead of one verra big plate o' food, you get to choose from lotsa itty-bitty small plates o' food!"

"What type of food?"

Luigi gave the boggart a triumphant grin. "Pasta!"

Humfrey groaned. "Now, why doeshn't that come ash a shurprise?"

"An' the best of it is," continued Luigi, ushering Humfrey inside, "that I can change the sign without buyin' any more letters! LUIGI'S PASTA BAR – LUIGI'S TAPAS BAR. PASTA – TAPAS. I jus' changed the letter order, see?"

Hot Dog, the overgrown canine who pulled Luigi's pizza delivery cart, looked up as they entered the restaurant and gave a tentative yap, but seeing that the visitor was only Humfrey, settled down again. Humfrey gazed at Luigi's new décor without enthusiasm.

"You got flowersh on the table," he said accusingly.

"The flowers is for ambience," Luigi told him with dignity.

"Mosht of the lowlifes who eat here will probably think they're for startersh. What'sh with the checked tableclothsh?" Clicking his tongue, Humfrey hopped on to a cane-backed chair (his legs didn't reach the floor) and picked up a large, flimsy sheet of paper. "And what'sh thish?"

"Tha's bran' new as well." Luigi gave him a conspiratorial wink. "It tells you everythin' tha's new. I's a news sheet."

Humfrey read the name of the paper from the top of the sheet. *"The Newsh of the Wood?"*

"Sure. Is'a give you all the news – an' livestock market prices, jousting results, recipes for spells…"

Humfrey sat bolt upright as a hissing, gurgling sound filled the restaurant. "You got a dragon in here or shomething?"

"Relax." Luigi bustled round behind the serving counter. "Is'a my milk-frothin' machine."

Humfrey stared at the hissing, spluttering device. "Thish ish another part of your new shtyle, ish it? It makes a noishe like a blocked privy. What doesh it do?"

"It makes milk all hot an' frothy." Luigi drew a cup of bubbling milk from the machine and brought it over to Humfrey's table. "The customers come in, an' read the paper, an' drink their nice frothy hot milk. Try some." He banged the cup down on the table.

Humfrey took a tentative sip of hot milk and gazed at the paper. His crumpled face took on a considering look. "I can't help thinking," he said slowly, "there'sh shomething misshing from thish experience." He put the cup down and stared at a pattern of black and white squares in a bottom corner of the news sheet. "Hey, what'sh thish?"

"Tha's a cross-rune puzzle. I's the…"

"…very latesht thing," completed Humfrey sourly. He read the first clue. "'Do wounded in city mix up? (3,8).' What'sh that all about?"

"It is quite simple, Master Boggart, for one with half a groat's worth of wit."

Humfrey looked up at the familiar voice, to find that the

other half of *Boggart and Rune: Inquestigators* had entered the restaurant. The Runemaster sat down opposite Humfrey and twiddled the end of his long, white beard between forefinger and thumb, watching with a half-smile as the boggart wrestled with the clue.

At length, Humfrey pushed the news sheet across the table to his partner. "OK, Runey. Let'sh asshume I don't have half a groat'sh worth of wit. Why don'cha shpell it out for me?"

"'Spell it out' is the operative phrase," said the Runemaster. "It's an anagram."

Humfrey's brow furrowed. "What'sh a nannygram?"

"Anagram. Thou mixest up the letters in the clue to make another word or phrase."

"Like pasta – tapas." Luigi winked at Humfrey. "Same letters, different order."

The boggart raised a puzzled eyebrow. "Why?"

"For the purposes of intellectual exercise," said the Runemaster loftily.

"For folksh with nothing better to do," pronounced Humfrey. "Who hash the time to make theshe thingsh up?"

The Runemaster suddenly became very interested in his beard and his twiddling got a lot faster. Humfrey gave him a knowing leer. "I thought it might be you."

The Runemaster sighed. "One has to do something to keep one's brain alert."

"It hash been kinda quiet round here," admitted Humfrey. He tapped the paper. "'Do wounded in city mix up? (3,8).' Sho what'sh the answer?"

"The number in the brackets tells thee how many words thou art looking for, and how many letters there are in each word; and 'mix up' tells thee the clue is an anagram; and the whole thing is the name of a city. Then 'tis just a matter of rearranging the letters of 'Do wounded in' and thou gettest..."

"Don't tell me! Don't tell me!" Humfrey closed his eyes in concentration for a few moments. Then he looked up and grinned. "Dun Indewood!"

"Exactly!" The Runemaster gave Humfrey a sly look. "And if the clue was, 'Thy huge Bertram fog', thou would'st get..."

"Humfrey the Boggart," supplied Luigi. He and the Runemaster roared with laughter. Humfrey's eyes narrowed.

"Right," he said menacingly. "And if the clue wash, 'Hi! Lug in a fat parasite', you'd get Luigi the Pastafarian!" Luigi stopped laughing. "Or if it wash, 'Erase Mr Nut', you'd get..."

The Runemaster coughed loudly. "Well, I have no more time to waste on these frivolities—"

He broke off as the door flew open and a small whirlwind shot into the restaurant, flapping the new checked tablecloths and tearing petals from Luigi's flowers. Hot Dog went into a frenzy of barking. When the dust had settled, Tym stood before them.

As Luigi quieted his excited dog, the Runemaster eyed Tym sternly. "What dost thou here, Master Whizzard? I thought thou wast engaged in delivering messages."

"I wast," panted Tym. "I mean, I was. Something came up..."

Luigi's milk-frothing machine had to be refilled twice while Tym told his story. By the time he had finished, everyone was looking grave and Humfrey was rubbing his chin thoughtfully.

"If Will and Rose are in danger," said the Runemaster, "we must act at once. Yet I would know more before we proceed."

"I can't tell you any more," said Tym. "You'd have to talk to the Dreamwalker."

Humfrey scowled. "Yeah? And how do you proposhe we do that?"

"It's perfectly simple," said Tym persuasively. "You just have to go to sleep. He'll do the rest."

"But it'sh barely lunch time!" protested Humfrey.

Luigi grinned. "What we need," he said decisively, "is a siesta."

"What," demanded Humfrey suspiciously, "is a shieshta?"

"Ol' Pastafarian custom," Luigi told him cheerfully. "Leave it all to Luigi. You're gonna love it..."

"How do you scratch your nose in these things?" demanded Rose.

Will looked at the chains fixing their feet to the floor of

the cell, and the manacles holding their arms above their heads, and sighed. "You don't." Rose, arching her back in a vain attempt at bringing her face within scratching distance of her hand, gave up, panting. She glared at Will, as if her predicament were his fault.

"Look on the bright side," said Will. "As dungeons go, this one isn't bad." He gazed at the large brass oil lamps whose light, flickering on the low arched roof and stone walls, gave their cell an inappropriately cosy atmosphere.

"Heavens, no!" said the Harp with heavy irony. It jangled discordantly, rattling its fetters. "These chains are as light as a feather."

"You're so right," agreed Rose. "This stone floor is positively comfy, and I daresay the rat that's sniffing round my feet will turn out to be really cuddly when I get to know him." She kicked out as viciously as her chains allowed and grinned at the resulting ratty squeak.

Will knew things were bad if Rose and the Harp had ganged up against him, but he ploughed on, "I mean, compared to the ones in Dun Indewood. It's clean, there are no skeletons, and I can't see any instruments of torture..."

"A regular home from home," needled the Harp. "If we had a few scatter cushions, a potted plant and a sampler saying *Dungeon, Sweet Dungeon*, you'd hardly know we were..." he paused for a second then screamed, "...incarcerated in an escape-proof cell facing something that is supposed to be worse than a horrible death!"

Will sighed. "Trying to keep your spirits up is a waste of time, isn't it?"

"Yup."

"What I don't understand," said Rose, "is why they're so keen on blaming us for this Knyghtmare. I mean, they're all out on their feet. Whatever's happening here must have started way before we arrived, so how do they make out it's all our fault?"

"That's humans for you," said the Harp. "They have to blame somebody, and they don't want to blame themselves. We're strangers, so they blame us."

"Or," said Will slowly, "we're being blamed to divert attention from the real culprit."

Rose stared at him. "What do you mean? This Knyghtmare, whatever it is, is the real culprit."

Will shook his head. "Think about it. Tym told us about the Dreamwalker. Now, a power that exists to reward good dreams and send bad ones to people with a guilty conscience, that makes sense. But a power that exists simply to send bad dreams to everyone, whether they've been good or bad, and drive them insane – what's the point of that? No. There's a nasty, clever, devious mind at work here. That almost certainly means a human mind."

The Harp gave Will a startled look. "Hey, what's this – we're singing from the same song sheet! I think humans are the pits, but I didn't expect to hear it from you!"

"I know exactly what humans are capable of," said Will grimly. "I *am* one—"

He broke off as the heavily barred door crashed open. There was a cry of "In you go!" as a blur of yellow and red shot through the opening, hit the hard marble floor and went, "Oof!"

"Hello, Scrape," said Rose brightly.

"That's all we need," moaned the Harp. "And me without my earplugs."

The jester scrambled to his feet, brushed down his parti-coloured costume and cuddled his stick with its doll's head. "Villains," he cried, shaking his fist and stamping his feet in impotent fury. "Bullies! Ruffians! You'll regret this later!"

The commander of the palace guard thrust his head round the door and leered at Scrape. "Maybe, O Jester. But right now I'm enjoying it. Laugh this off!"

The head withdrew; the door slammed shut. The jester gave a huge sigh and sank cross-legged on to the stone floor. There was a silence. Will examined their new cellmate carefully. The oddly-coloured outfit and close-fitting cap drew attention away from its wearer, as if the jester's clothes *were* his personality, and it was difficult to think of Scrape as a person at all. Feeling sorry for the jester, and vaguely guilty, Will said, "What are you doing here? Are you a prisoner?"

Scrape jerked his head. "Sorry, didn't hear you. Did you say something?"

Will repeated the question and the jester nodded mournfully. "The Vizier had me arrested. He doesn't appreciate my jesting."

"A man with taste," muttered the Harp. Will aimed a kick at it, but the chains on his ankles brought his foot up short. The Harp snickered.

"This happens all the time," said Scrape glumly. "I do my humble best to entertain the court, Vizier Shaman has me arrested and thrown in the dungeons, and when the Emir finds out he orders my release. Until the next time..."

There was a heavy silence. Then Scrape looked up with an expression of desperate gaiety. "Shall I divert you with riddles and shafts of wit, to pass the weary hours?"

"No!" said Rose and the Harp together. Will gave the jester an encouraging look, but his heart sank.

"Come, let us be merry!" Scrape leapt to his feet and cut a half-hearted caper. "Riddle me this. What goes up, but never comes down?"

"Your age," said Rose immediately.

The jester's face fell, but he rallied. "What gets wetter as it dries?"

"A towel," said the Harp with an elaborate yawn.

An edge of panic crept into Scrape's voice. "Then tell me this: what kind of bow can never be tied?"

"A rainbow," said Rose. "My grandmama told me that one."

Tears were welling in the jester's eyes. "What has teeth but cannot bite?"

"A comb," said Rose and the Harp simultaneously.

The jester gave a stifled scream. "What always goes to bed with its shoes on?"

"A horse," drawled the Harp. "I know mountains that aren't as old as this material. Listen, beanpole, you want to hear some really terrific career advice? Quit showbiz right now, because funny you ain't."

Scrape slumped. "That's what everyone says," he sniffed. Then he brightened slightly. "Except the Emir. He thinks I'm hilarious."

"Yes," said Rose bitterly, "but he thinks we're criminals, which shows how good a judge *he* is."

The jester eyed them doubtfully. "Are you not evil spies and enchanters?"

"Of course we're not." Rose controlled her temper with an effort. "Listen, if you really want to help us, suppose you tell us what's going on around here?" Scrape looked doubtful. "For instance," Rose insisted, "why did everyone in the court start climbing the walls when the Vizier read Will's dream and that black Knyght thing appeared?" She turned her attention to Will. "You saw it first back in the Forest, didn't you? I remember you asking me whether I'd seen it too." Will nodded. Rose turned back to the jester. "Scrape, this black Knyght – is that the Knyghtmare we keep hearing about?"

The jester put his head in his hands. "Yes. For many days now, the Knyghtmare has ridden through our dreams in the form of a Knyght, armoured in black, on a black horse. And in his train he brings dreams... such dreams." Scrape shuddered.

The Harp's face wore an unusually thoughtful expression. "I don't get it. All humans dream, right? And some of those dreams have got to be bad?"

Rose nodded. "I've had bad dreams from time to time – dreams about falling, and monsters under the bed. Of course, in the Dark Forest, sometimes there really *were* monsters under the bed..."

"I know what you mean," said Will. "I have bad dreams too. Everybody does – though, come to think of it, the nearer we've got to here, the worse the dreams have become. But what's so terrible about the dreams the Knyghtmare brings?"

"Try going to sleep," said Scrape grimly. "You'll find out." Seeing that Will and Rose looked abashed, the jester continued. "You don't understand – you don't know what it's like. When our dreams were sent by the Dreamwalker, sometimes those dreams were bad – when we'd done something nasty, or unkind – but usually we knew what we'd done and we knew we deserved the bad dream. Or if we didn't understand our dreams, we could go to the Dream Readers and they'd tell us what they meant. And if we'd done kind or generous things, the Dreamwalker would send us good dreams. But then..." Scrape's body shivered and his voice lowered to a whisper, "the Knyghtmare came."

Will's heart pounded uncomfortably against his ribs as he remembered his meetings with the black Knyght. "Have *you* seen him?"

Scrape nodded grimly. "Oh yes. All those who dream see him. That is why people avoid sleep as long as they can, as they would avoid fire, plague or death. For now *all* our dreams are bad. The Knyghtmare takes the kindest thoughts, the most generous deeds, the most selfless actions – and twists them into their opposites. Its victims suffer excesses of fear, guilt, remorse, until eventually they come to believe that everything they have ever done was vain, cruel and selfish. And the dreams! Torments unimaginable; imps, demons, insects that sting and bite and never let go; great beasts that fight and tear!"

"It sounds terrible," said Rose.

"Yes," said Scrape simply. "Moreover, some of the dreams are of things that have not yet happened – and they always come true, no matter what the dreamer does to try to prevent them." He gave Will and Rose a conspiratorial wink. "I knew a man who dreamt that he would fall to his death. He had his bed moved to the ground floor. He even had the stairs in his own home walled up in case he should sleepwalk. He refused to go anywhere near a balcony. One day, while taking a detour down a dark alley to avoid a flight of steps, he tumbled headfirst down a well and drowned. Well, you've got to laugh, haven't you?" Scrape registered Will and Rose's appalled expressions and sighed. "No, you're right. Dreams like that are the cruelest of all. But that's why in Beau Revere now, everyone will do almost anything to stay awake. Everyone from the Emir to the lowest beggar."

Rose nodded encouragingly. "Tell us about the Emir and the court."

Hesitantly, Scrape said, "Well, the Emir is the ruler of the city, of course, and the man with the black robes and no appreciation of the jester's art..." Here the Harp guffawed and Scrape pointedly ignored it. "...is the Grand Vizier and Chief Dream Reader, Shaman al'Seer. It is said that he is betrothed to Princess Shayde, the daughter of Emir Raj. They are to marry when she comes of age."

Rose's eyebrows shot up. "You mean the bald man with the robes and the girl who was kneeling beside the Emir's throne? The one who wanted him to burn us?" Scrape nodded. "And how does Shayde feel about that?"

Scrape hesitated; then he murmured, "It is said that she doesn't like the idea one little bit."

"I'm not surprised," said Will a little too quickly. "He's a bit past it, isn't he?"

Rose gave Will a penetrating stare. "Oho!"

Will looked blank. "Oho, what?"

"Nothing. Just 'Oho!'"

Scrape shrugged. "Well, anyway, I think I've told you everything."

Rose gave the jester an appraising look. "Not quite," she said. "You haven't told us about yourself. No offence, but you don't look as if you belong here."

"I don't," agreed Scrape. "I was born and brought up in a city far from here."

"Dinas Ruined?" said Rose eagerly. "We've been there."

"No, no," said Scrape hastily. "Not Dinas Ruined. It's a long way from here – you wouldn't know it. Anyway, I became court jester to the lord of the city. I was a great favourite and went with him everywhere. But one day, as we were travelling through the Forest, we were set upon by outlaws. Our guards were killed, our wagons fired. Somehow, I escaped, and wandered through the Forest for many days before I found my way here. The people took me in – and again I became a favourite, but only of Emir Raj." Scrape sighed heavily. "Perhaps my humour doesn't travel well. I don't think anyone else likes my jokes at all."

Will and Rose exchanged glances. Scrape hadn't come from Dun Indewood, or from Dinas Ruined. That meant there must be more cities out there in the Dark Forest!

But before Rose could question the jester further, the bolts on the door were shot back and a squad of hollow-eyed, yawning guards arrived.

The commander pointed at Scrape. "You! You're released. Emir's orders." He jerked a thumb towards the open door.

Scrape beamed, and nodded to Will and Rose. "Told you." He made for the door, pausing to say to the guard commander, "Would'st hear a merry quip, friend?"

"That depends," said the commander. "Would'st have me smear you with honey and stake you to an anthill until the flesh is stripped from your bones and your skeleton is left to bleach in the merciless glare of the sun?"

The Harp sniggered. Scrape's face fell. "There's no need to be nasty," he said in injured tones. At the door, he turned to Will and Rose, said, "See? Nobody appreciates me," and shuffled out.

The guard commander took a key ring from his waist and set about releasing his prisoners from their chains. Rose said in hope rather than expectation, "I don't suppose the Emir has ordered us to be set free, too?"

The commander gave a harsh chuckle. "No such luck, O stranger. I'm here to take you to the Court of Dreams."

CHAPTER SIX

Of Knyghtmare Confusions and foregone
Conclusions.

Back In Dun Indewood, Luigi was counting the empties.

"Six flagons o' wine... forty-eight tapas dishes, tha's twelve each... a coupl'a loaves o' bread to mop up the juices..." The pastafarian gave a calculating nod. "Yep. Tha' should just about do it. If that lot has'n made us sleepy, nothin' will."

Humfrey massaged his groaning belly. "Did you have to use sho much chilli?"

"Is'a good for you," Luigi told him sternly. "It cleans out the blood."

"Feelsh like that'sh not all it'sh going to clean out,"

muttered Humfrey darkly; but no one heard. Tym, lying on the bench where Luigi's customers waited for tables to become vacant, was already snoring. The Runemaster's eyelids were drooping and, as Humfrey watched, the old wizard's head sank forward on to his folded arms. Luigi, who was used to taking a siesta whenever opportunity offered, settled himself on to an overstuffed footstool, braced his back against the wall, threw his apron over his head and soon began to snore too. Even Hot Dog was asleep. Humfrey felt his own eyelids growing hot and heavy. He settled back in his chair, stretched his legs out across another, and began to doze...

...and found himself on the Dreamwalker's plain. The Runemaster, Luigi and Tym were already there, staring up in awe at the gigantic shadowy figure.

Then the Runemaster stepped forward and bowed as to an equal. Humfrey knew that the old wizard had outfaced dragons and trolls in his time. Even so, he was impressed.

"I would know more of the power of dreams," said the Runemaster calmly.

In answer, the Dreamwalker gestured and a scene appeared before their eyes.

A woman was reclining on a soft couch. Her eyes were troubled. A man wearing robes of deep blue sat cross-legged on a cushion beside the couch, watching her with an expression of detached interest.

"O Dream Reader," the woman said in a tremulous voice, *"I have a dream that troubles me. I would know its meaning."*

The man nodded. Without speaking, he indicated a

transparent globe of some crystalline substance. (*"A dream viewer,"* explained the Dreamwalker.) The woman placed her right hand on the surface of the dome, the man his left. Then the man moved his right hand in a slow, complex gesture. The woman's eyes closed. For a moment, nothing further happened – then clouds began to form in the centre of the globe. A few seconds more, and the clouds began to clear.

Two baby birds lay in a nest. The mother bird flew down and fed the smaller bird. The larger baby was jealous. When the mother flew away again, it attacked the smaller bird, pecking and heaving with its stubby wings, until the smaller bird tumbled from the nest. It lay on the ground far below, cheeping feebly.

The globe clouded again and became dark. The Dream Reader removed his hand from the globe and gestured again. The woman awoke.

"You have a sister," said the Dream Reader in a dispassionate voice. The woman bowed her head. *"You have done her wrong because you believed that your mother favoured her. You have come to understand that you were unjust to your sister. The memory of your treatment of her fills you with guilt. This is the meaning of your dream."*

The woman looked up. *"How must I make amends?"*

The Dream Reader shook his head. *"That is not for me to say. You must decide your course."*

The woman nodded and thanked the Dream Reader. The vision faded. Once again, Humfrey and his companions found themselves on the Dreamwalker's empty plain.

The Dreamwalker said, *"Before the mists came to drive me from Beau Revere, such dream readings were made there many times a day, by hundreds of Dream Readers trained for that purpose. I watched over all my people at all times. I saw into the innermost secrets of their hearts. I sent them dreams that would make them examine their feelings and their actions. Those who had done good were rewarded with sweet dreams. But those who had done evil had no refuge. They might escape detection. They might escape justice. They might escape prison. But they could not escape my dreams."*

"And who would do wrong in thy city, knowing what torments awaited them when they slept?" said the Runemaster quietly. *"It is a great power that thou hast, for good – or ill."*

"For good," said the Dreamwalker coldly. The great being was evidently not used to being questioned, however courteously. *"For good only, be assured."*

The Runemaster inclined his head. *"By thee, I am sure it is. But suppose another had such power. Might it not be used for evil?"* The Dreamwalker remained silent. *"Supposing,"* the Runemaster continued, *"that some creature – driven perhaps by greed, vengefulness or spite – discovered how to wield the power of dreams. Might such a creature not twist that power to evil? And doing so, challenge thy mastery?"*

Tym gazed at the Runemaster with an expression of horror. Humfrey nodded grimly. Luigi shook his head and tutted.

The Dreamwalker's expression was unreadable.

"And were that so, would not thy adversary, confident in his power, seek to attack thee in the heart of thy realm – with such results as thou hast described to us?"

Slowly, reluctantly, the Dreamwalker said, *"Indeed, that is what I fear..."*

As if in response to the shadowy creature's sombre mood, heaving clouds began to mass above them.

In a hollow voice, Tym said, *"Those who corrupt dreams find them turning into nightmares."* He looked up at the Dreamwalker. *"I reminded you of those words when we met in the Forest – and you said, no, they would find them turning into the Knyghtmare. What did you mean?"*

The Dreamwalker shook his great head. *"I do not know for certain. But for the past year, before the mists came to banish me from Beau Revere, my people began to have dreams – evil dreams – which were none of my sending. At some point in every such dream, the dreamer would suffer an attack from a Knyght, dressed all in black, upon a black horse..."*

"I saw it!" Tym cried excitedly. *"In the Forest. It attacked me too."*

"The Dream Readers of my city began to refer to the attacker as the Knyghtmare," murmured the Dreamwalker. *"In the form of this black Knyght, it rides the storm of evil dreams sent to plague my people. Yet it is not an elemental, a creature of magic, as I am. Therefore it must be the creation of some being – a human, I deem – who has learnt to harness the power of dreams to some fell purpose."*

The clouds hung lower now, denser and more menacing.

"If you have guessed aright," said the Runemaster, *"and there is a human in Beau Revere who has created the Knyghtmare and who now controls it, Rose and Will are in great*

danger every minute they remain in the City of Dreams. We must act at once!"

As he spoke, lightning flashed across the plain, followed by a monstrous peal of thunder, and the heavens opened. Rain fell in torrents, drenching the unhappy companions...

...and Humfrey jerked awake to a world of wetness which, he realised a moment later, was caused by a slobbering tongue licking his face enthusiastically.

"Hot Dog!" roared Humfrey, pushing Luigi's drooling canine companion aside. "Cut that out!" He stared around, blinking Hot Dog's slobber from his eyes. The Runemaster, Tym and Luigi were all wiping themselves with napkins having evidently already received similar treatment. Hot Dog sat on his haunches in the middle of the restaurant, panting and looking very pleased with himself.

Humfrey reached for one of the brightly checked tablecloths. Ignoring Luigi's protests, he tugged sharply – and the cloth slid smoothly from under the central vase of flowers, leaving it standing on the table without a petal out of place.

Scrubbing vigorously at his dripping face, Humfrey said, "OK, Runey, you shaid yourshelf it was too quiet around here. Sheemsh like we have a little trip in front of ush."

"But we don't even know where Beau Revere is," protested Tym.

"I believe we do," said the Runemaster. "On one of the old maps in the castle archive, there is a city marked to the southeast of Dun Indewood, not too far from where Tym says he met the Dreamwalker. The name has been nibbled away by vermin, but I should be surprised if it were not the place we seek."

"Then we'd better get going," said Humfrey, his boggart tidiness kicking in as he busily collected slobbery tablecloths, towels and napkins and looked around for Luigi's linen basket. "If we're gonna help Will and Rose, we've got shome inqueshtigating to do."

"Thou meanest," said the Runemaster pointedly, "that *thou* hast some inquestigating to do. Time is of the essence, and it would take far too long for both of us to travel to Beau Revere. Thou art on thine own."

"What?" Humfrey dropped his bundle and stared at his partner. "I don't get it. Why would it take ush longer to go together than it would for me to go by myshelf?"

The Runemaster looked steadily at Humfrey, then he turned and stared at Tym in a significant sort of way. Then he turned back to Humfrey and raised his eyebrows.

Humfrey's ruddy face turned pale. He started to back away. "Oh, no." He held up his hands in a gesture of refusal. "Not a chance. You have to be kiddin' me. Don't even think about it..."

The Court of Dreams was, in its way, even more imposing than the Emir's audience room. Every inch of its walls was richly decorated with panels of rare and scented woods, elaborately carved. The floors glittered with mosaics, the ceiling was frosted with ornate plaster work, highlighted with gold and silver leaf, topaz, garnet and lapis lazuli. Colonnaded galleries around three sides of the court room were crowded with dignitaries. The Emir sat in the light of a great jewelled window, on an ornate golden throne so large that his pudgy figure looked no bigger than that of a small boy. Shayde sat demurely on a footstool beside the throne, and Scrape hovered uncertainly in the background. Below the throne, a row of court officials in rich robes were scribbling furiously on parchment. They sagged into vast velvet cushions, fighting against the sleep they so desperately craved. Behind them was a row of servants armed with long sticks, ready to prod any dozing official, and behind them, another row of servants, similarly armed, whose job seemed to be to keep the first row of prodders awake.

Will (clutching the Harp) and Rose were unceremoniously ushered in just as the previous trial was reaching its climax. As they were being forced on to seats at the very back of the court, Will became aware of the Vizier, standing on a marble platform with a gleaming, golden handrail. He was pointing an accusatory finger at a man in a kind of bell-shaped cage surrounded by guards, who was staring about with an air of sullen defiance.

"O prisoner," the Vizier intoned, "you have been found guilty of all charges. Hear now the divine justice of your sovereign lord, His Most Phantasmagorical and Deluded Highness, King of Shadows, Visionary of Visionaries, Most Puissant Fantasist of the Intangible Dominions, Hereditary

Grand Hallucinator, Emperor of the Chimerical and Dread Sovereign Lord of the Insubstantial Realm, Emir Raj!"

The Emir drew himself up. "Yes. Absolutely. You've been a very bad, naughty man, and your punishment shall be...". After several seconds of frenzied thought, he mopped his face and said, "...whatever our Grand Vizier thinks is appropriate."

The prisoner gripped the bars of the cage and glared defiantly at the Vizier. "Well, noble Vizier. What is it to be? Am I to be beheaded? Hanged? Burnt at the stake? I defy you! Do your worst!"

"No," said the Vizier softly. "Your punishment shall be..." he paused "...that you shall be taken from this court to a place of repose, and there you shall be made to lie in a warm bed, with many soft pillows, and given a potion that shall send you into a deep sleep from which you will not wake, let your dreams be what they may."

The prisoner's air of defiance disappeared as quickly as a raindrop in a desert. "No!" he gasped, his face suffused with terror. "Mercy! Anything but that! The axe... the noose... I beg you, anything!" At a signal from the Vizier, he was dragged from his cage by the guards and hauled away in chains, his shrieks of despair continuing to echo around the court long after he had vanished from sight.

The Vizier bowed to the Emir, then immediately cried, "Bring forth the strangers!" He clapped his hands and a brass gong echoed round the court.

"I *really* hate it when they do that," muttered the Harp as his strings jangled once again.

Will and Rose were hustled forward and thrust into the bell-shaped cage, which was evidently there for prisoners on trial. The onlookers all craned over as far as they dared to get a sight of the evil enchanters who were, rumour said, responsible for the plight of their city.

The Vizier stepped forward, but before he could speak, the Harp struck three dramatic chords. "I demand the right to represent myself and my clients here," he said loftily.

"Be silent," barked the Vizier, "or I will demand an axe!"

"Good point, well argued," said the Harp. It turned to Will and Rose. "Sorry people, you're on your own."

The Vizier turned on Will and Rose. "Transgressors!" he cried. "When you are found guilty, you will be taken away to a place of repose where you will sleep, perchance to dream."

"Tough luck, folks," said the Harp, winking at Will and Rose. It turned to the Vizier with a triumphant look. "You can't get *me* that way, big shot. I don't dream."

"As for your vile instrument," said the Vizier, "possessed, as it undoubtedly is, by an evil jinnee, it shall be burnt."

"Oh, rats!" moaned the Harp. "Not fair! Anyhow, what's with the *when* we're found guilty? Shouldn't that be *if*?"

A roar of incredulous laughter echoed around the court. The Emir howled with mirth, his turban slipping sideways over one ear, and Shayde's lip curled. Even the Vizier permitted himself a frosty smile.

The Harp gave a twanging sigh. "Well, I guess that answers *that* question."

The Vizier held up one hand and the laughter died.

Turning to the cage, he said, "Wretched malefactors, you are strangers to our city, which is in itself a grave breach of our laws in time of crisis. The verdict is not in doubt; this trial is a necessary formality. We must follow the due form of law, or we should be no better than barbarians. Only the sentence remains to be decided. Have you anything to say in your own defence?"

"Yes."

Will gaped at Rose, who had spoken. What could she possibly say? They'd obviously already been judged guilty.

The Harp hissed, "Go for it! Beg for our lives. Give them some stuff about how you were orphans led astray, that you're just misunderstood and society is to blame." It began to strum a heart-rending little tune.

Rose ignored both the Harp and Will. "Your Majesty," she cried in ringing tones that carried to every corner of the vast room. "My Lord Vizier! We do not beg. We offer you a bargain!"

There were shocked gasps at the temerity of Rose's words. The Harp broke off in a jangling discord. "That's it. We are soooo dead..."

The Vizier grew purple with rage, but controlled himself with an obvious effort. In mocking tones, he said, "Indeed. And what bargain does this vagabond stranger offer the court of His Most Phantasmagorical and Deluded Highness, King of Shadows, Visionary of Visionaries, Most Puissant Fantasist of the Intangible Dominions, Hereditary Grand Hallucinator, Emperor of the Chimerical and Dread Sovereign Lord of the Insubstantial Realm, Emir Raj?"

Will waited for Rose's answer with bated breath. He'd been wondering that himself.

"Just this," said Rose in a clear, calm voice. "Spare our lives, and we will undertake to defeat the Knyghtmare, restore the Dreamwalker and save your city!"

CHAPTER SEVEN

How the Boggart got the Hump, and Will was made an offer he Couldn't Refuse.

"The moment thou arrivest at Beau Revere," the Runemaster told Humfrey, "thou shalt be in grave danger. I would be on my guard, if I were thee."

The boggart gave his partner a reproving look. "For two groatsh you *can* be me, Runey. I don't recall volunteering for thish assignment."

The Runemaster let out an exasperated groan. "How many more times? It *has* to be thee. The only way thou canst reach Beau Revere in time is if Tym carries thee at Whizzard speed."

Tym gave the unhappy boggart an apologetic look.

"Sorry," he said, "but I haven't got any Whizzard potion to give you, and the Dreamwalker is too busy fighting off the Knyghtmare to make any more."

"I shtill don't shee why I can't go on dragon-back," said Humfrey stubbornly.

"We have been through this! It would take too long. Tym would have to travel to the Ragged Mountain to find Greywing, and then they would have to come back here. Days would be lost."

Tym nodded. "And I'm not even sure Greywing would come."

Humfrey snorted. "Sure he would. He hash a lot of reshpect for Will."

"I know. But last time I went to see him and his hoard-mate, I'm pretty sure Darkscale was in a..." Tym coughed. "...delicate condition, if you know what I mean."

"You mean they's expectin' the flappin' of tiny wings?" A sentimental look spread across Luigi's ample face. "Aaaaaahhh! Tha's'a nice."

"Yeah, that'sh great newsh," agreed Humfrey gloomily. "The only thing that shtopsh me being ecstatic with joy ish that it meansh I'm shtuck with Mishter Shpeedy. Have you sheen how fasht thish guy travelsh?"

"I am surprised at thee," said the Runemaster loftily. "Wouldst thou be ruled by thy fear of moderate speed and a little temporary discomfort?"

"You left out 'looking like a shap'," snapped Humfrey. "Hey, Runey, if you think ridin' piggyback on Greashed Lightning here ish such a great idea, why don't you do it?"

Tym had had enough. "In the first place," he snapped, "because the Dreamwalker asked for you. And in the second place, because the Runemaster is too tall, and you're..." The penetrating nature of Humfrey's stare finally got through to Tym and his voice tailed off.

"You wanna complete that thought, kid?" demanded the boggart in a dangerously quiet voice.

"I shouldn't," Luigi nudged Tym and went on in a confidential whisper, "He's verra self-conscious about his size."

"We waste time in futile wrangling," said the Runemaster tetchily. "If it were done when 'tis done, t'were well it were done quickly."

Humfrey stared at his partner. "What the blishtering blue blazes ish that shupposed to mean?" The Runemaster scowled. "OK, OK, I'm going." Humfrey shouldered the pack of food that Luigi had prepared to see him and Tym through their journey, and climbed on to a chair. Tym bent his knees and reached behind him to take Humfrey's weight.

The boggart hesitated. Then he tapped Tym on the shoulder.

"Jusht one thing," he told the Whizzard in confidential tones. "If you shtart shinging *Ride a Cock Horse to Brambley Crossh* or *The Wheelsh on the Cart go Round and Round*, or any other dumb shong parents shing to their kidsh when they give them a ride, just to be a wise guy, you are gonna be *soooooooo* sorry..."

Will stared at Rose in horrified amazement. "Are you out of your tree?"

Rose glared. "Sssssh!"

"How are we supposed to save the city?" demanded Will in a harsh whisper.

"I don't know."

"Then why did you just tell them we could?"

"It buys us some time."

"Time to think about all the horrible things they're going to do to us when they find out we can't? Oh, good."

The Vizier evidently shared Will's doubts. "You lie, O woman," he snarled. "In the blackness of your heart, you lie. In the cunning of your mind, you lie. With your tongue, through your lips and in your teeth, you lie."

"He's got you there," hissed the Harp. "He may be a ruthless, inhuman, power-crazed sourpuss, but you have to admit, he's a terrific judge of character."

The Vizier, glowering, cried, "The soft beds and plump cushions await. Take them away."

"Wait!" Ignoring Shaman's furious glare, Shayde turned swiftly and knelt before the Emir's throne. "O my Father," she said softly, "would it not be wise to consider the strangers' offer?"

"I don't see why," huffed the Emir. "She's probably fibbing anyway."

"O my Father, your wisdom falls as dew upon the parched earth," said Shayde insincerely. "Yet, reflect. Your city stands on the brink of ruin. Your people stagger and faint from want of sleep, or else fall under the dominion of the Knyghtmare and run mad. Farmers set not their hands to the plough, nor hunters to the bow. Soon we shall face famine. If these strangers claim they can help us overcome our terrible adversary, should we not offer them the opportunity to prove themselves?"

The Harp's wooden brow furrowed. "What's Miss Smarty-Pants trying to pull? A minute ago she wanted to turn us into cinders!"

"And if it turns out they can't help us after all," Shayde concluded matter-of-factly, "you can always deal with them later."

The Emir, who had listened to his daughter's appeal with pursed lips, brightened visibly. "That's true. What say you, Vizier?"

The Vizier was clearly furious at the intervention, but he kept his temper. He bowed courteously to Shayde. "Sooner or later, their fate will be the same. Let the strangers make good their boast, by all means." He gave Will a particularly nasty look. "If they can."

"Very well." The Emir drew himself up regally and completely failed to look impressive. "Strangers, we decree that you shall do your utmost to rid our city and dominions of the presence of the Knyghtmare. If you succeed, you shall be pardoned and rewarded with your weight in gold..." The Vizier coughed warningly. "...Well, quite a lot of gold." The Vizier coughed again. "Some gold at least?" The Vizier gave a reluctant nod. "Good! But if you fail..." The Emir spluttered for a moment or so, trying to think of a more horrible punishment than the one Will and Rose were already facing. Failing, he concluded lamely, "Well, you'd better not, that's all."

"Yet, my father," said Shayde in such a respectful voice that the Vizier instantly gave her a highly suspicious look, "there is more to be said. By immemorial custom, if your dominions, being in danger, are saved by a young man of courage, resource and daring, you must offer him your eldest daughter in marriage." She gave Will a melting look.

Will gaped at Shayde and gasps of shock went up from the assembled courtiers. The Vizier turned purple and seemed to be about to explode with rage. The Emir gave a cry of dismay. "But *you* are my eldest daughter, and already betrothed to my Vizier. You are to marry him when you come of age." He gave Will a look of pure horror. "And he is... so lank of hair... and uncouth... a barbarian..."

The Harp leered at Will. "So that's what the minx was after. Hubba-hubba-hubba! Nice goin', lover boy."

Rose gazed at Shayde with an expression of utmost loathing. The Emir's daughter was staring defiantly at the Vizier, lips set in a mocking half-smile. Rose turned to Will. "What are you smirking about?" she demanded furiously.

Will, who had allowed himself a brief, rueful smile at the sight of Rose's discomfiture, objected, "I wasn't smirking."

"Don't give me that. I know a smirk when I see one."

The Emir and the Vizier were now arguing in furious whispers. At length, Emir Raj looked up and clapped his hands. "Enough!" he squeaked. "So be it!" The Vizier opened his mouth to protest, but the Emir cut him off with an uncharacteristically sharp gesture. "I am sorry, Shaman, but a custom is a custom." Looking at Will as though he were some crawling thing he'd just found in his salad, the Emir said, "Succeed in destroying the Knyghtmare, barbarian, and you shall have my daughter's hand in marriage."

"Just the hand?" muttered Rose, staring at Shayde as though willing her to burst into flames where she stood.

"Very well," hissed the Vizier, "yet the patience of His Most Phantasmagorical and Deluded Highness, King of Shadows, Visionary of Visionaries, Most Puissant Fantasist of the Intangible Dominions, Hereditary Grand Hallucinator, Emperor of the Chimerical and Dread Sovereign Lord of the Insubstantial Realm, Emir Raj, is not unlimited."

The Emir looked puzzled. "Isn't it?"

"It must be pretty good, if he has to listen to this rigmarole every time his name's mentioned," whispered the Harp.

"Therefore," continued the Vizier, "the strangers must destroy this Knyghtmare by sunset tomorrow or be delivered up as its victims." He directed a stony look at the captain of the palace guard. "Guards, see to it that they do not leave the city."

There was an awkward pause. Everyone looked at the Emir, who gave a start. "Oh – is that it? Erm... fine! Good. You are dismissed." He waved Will and Rose away as though they were annoying insects. The Vizier gave Will a murderous glare and signalled to four guards, who opened the door of the cage. Still carrying the Harp, Will bowed. Rose stuck her nose in the air and turned on her heel. Will followed. The guards fell into step behind them as they left the throne room.

When the great doors had closed, Rose rounded on Will. "You make me sick!"

Will stared at her. "What? Why?"

"I saw you making sheep's eyes at that... that hussy!"

"Who, me?"

"Yes, you!"

"Couldn't take his eyes off her," confirmed the Harp, who never missed an opportunity to stir up trouble. It gave Will a contemptuous look. "Heartbreaker!"

"Look," said Will desperately, "I didn't ask Shayde—" He got no further.

"Oh, it's 'Shayde' now, is it?" Rose folded her arms and glared at Will. "Before long, it'll be 'dear Shayde' and then 'Shayde, sweetie', and after that we're into areas that are too disgusting to contemplate..."

"It's not like that," said Will, trying to pacify Rose. "There's no need for you to be jealous—" Instantly, he knew he'd made another mistake.

"Jealous? Why should I be jealous? I'm not jealous! I just can't for the life of me understand what she sees in you, that's all. I mean, just look at you!"

Will bristled. "What about me?"

"Well, let's face it, you're no oil painting, are you? You're barely a wood cut!"

"Oh, thanks very much."

"You look as if you've been dragged through a hedge backwards…"

"I have. Several hedges, not to mention bushes, streams and bramble patches. Mostly by you…"

"Don't interrupt. Your clothes look as if they've been slept in…"

"They have been slept in…"

"…and your armour looks as if it's been sat on. By something heavy. With hygiene problems. And as for your face…"

"Oh boy," muttered the Harp, licking his lips. "This is gonna be good. I could sell tickets."

"…your best friends might call you handsome…"

"Well, thank you."

"…if you paid them a lot of money, but as far as anyone else is concerned, it's enough to frighten children. Eyebrows like giant hairy caterpillars."

Unconsciously, Will brushed back the hair that continually flopped into his eyes, trying at the same time to feel whether his eyebrows had grown during his travels. Realising what he was doing, he snatched his hand away.

"And shifty eyes," added the Harp. "Don't forget the shifty eyes."

Will glared at it. "Who asked you?"

"In any case," continued Rose, "she's a princess, and Scrape told us she already has a swain…"

"Yeah, but let's face it, her swain is a bit of a swine," said the Harp. "I hate to break up a really promising fight, but hasn't it occurred to you two dimwits what Daddy's little girl is really after?"

"Supposing you tell us," grated Rose.

"It's obvious! Remember what Scrape told us. She doesn't fancy the idea of getting hitched to old egg-head and she'll do anything to get his goat, even if it means cosying up with Sir Dripalot here..." Will squeezed the Harp until its frame creaked. "Ouch! What's the matter – you can't take a little constructive criticism?"

The light of battle faded from Rose's eyes. Thoughtfully, she said, "Yes. That would explain it."

Will fumed in silence. Why did Rose assume there was no chance that Shayde might just like him?

But a little voice in his mind agreed with Rose. Yes, very likely, isn't it, that someone like Shayde would fall head over heels in love with a pig herder's son who had never finished Knyght School and would never amount to anything...

Rose had recovered her composure. She gave Will an ironic curtsey. "All right, what do *you* suggest we do now, O infinitely-desirable-and-all-knowing-one?"

With studied casualness, Will said, "Well, I suppose we ought to find out what's happening here in Beau Revere."

Rose tilted her head to one side. "Oh, so we *are* going to investigate. Even though, according to you, we can't do anything?"

Will shrugged. "Like you said, it buys us time. Now we have a deadline."

The Harp gave a cackle. "*Dead*line is right. If you don't destroy the Knyghtmare – you're both dead!"

CHAPTER EIGHT

How Humfrey was taken for a Ride, and Will and Rose decided to round up the Usual Suspects.

"Aaaaaaaaaaaaarrrrrrrrrrrrrrggggggghhhhhhh!!!"

"I wish you'd stop screaming like that," Tym told Humfrey in aggrieved tones.

"OK, how about if I scream like this? Eeeeee eeerrrrrrrrrrrrggggggghh!!!"

"You're perfectly safe."

"Shure I am, and I'll go on being perfectly shafe right up to the moment you hit shomething. Aaaaaaaarrr rrrggghhh!!"

"See? You're getting used to moving this fast. Your screams are getting shorter."

"Aaaaaaaaaaaarrrrrrrrrrrrrrgggggghhhhhhh!!!"

"Why don't you close your eyes, if you're worried?"

"They *are* closed, and I'm *shtill* worried!" moaned Humfrey. "Do we have to go thish fast? Mind that tree!"

Tym, exasperated, slid to a halt, leaving a smoking furrow and scattering the dust and leaf mould of the Forest. Humfrey tumbled off his back and lay on the ground, moaning. Tym leant against a tree while the boggart reached inside his tunic, pulled out a metal flask, unscrewed the cap and took a generous swig.

"Riding on your back shtinksh," the boggart complained.

Tym summoned up all his reserves of patience. "Look, I only have three speeds: normal speed, which wouldn't get us to Beau Revere in time; Whizzard speed, where I move so fast nobody can see me; and in-between speed – I call it wind speed – where I move so fast that, for instance, I can run over a lake and not sink. That's the speed we've been going, and I promise you, I've covered hundreds of leagues through the Dark Forest and never hit anything yet."

"Maybe, but it'sh only a matter of time."

"It seems fast to you," Tym said reassuringly, "because you're used to normal speeds. I'm used to wind speed, maybe that's part of the magic – my reactions are faster or something. At any rate, I'm no more likely to run into anything than you would be if you went for a run in the Forest."

"Why would I want to go for a run in the Foresht?" Humfrey shook his head. "I don't get it. If your fashtesht shpeed is Whizzard shpeed, why don't we ushe that?"

"It depends on your point of view," explained Tym. "It's fastest from your point of view, but for me it's like walking through a world where everything but me has stopped. It takes ages in my time to get anywhere, even though for the rest of the world, very little time has passed."

Humfrey stared at him. "I wash with you right up until you shtarted talking."

Tym ignored this. "In any case, I've never tried carrying anybody at Whizzard speed. I don't know what would happen to you if the rest of the world was moving past you so fast you couldn't see it."

Humfrey shuddered. "OK, OK, you've made your point." Sighing, the boggart struggled to his feet. After a good deal of grunting, he managed to resettle himself on Tym's back.

"Ready?" Tym set off.

"Aaaaaaaaaaaarrrrrrrrrrrrrrggggggghhhhhhh!!!"

"...and this is the Market Square," said Scrape gloomily.

The jester had offered to show Will and Rose around the city. He'd explained that, owing to the Vizier's mood, he didn't think the court was the safest place for him to be at the moment. And so they had left the palace, with the guards following them like shadows. Scrape had insisted on leaving the Harp behind (much to its disgust) – the people of Beau Revere, he'd said, had enough to worry about without being visited by strange talking instruments possessed by demons.

Not, thought Will ruefully, that there were many people around anyway. The streets were empty, most of the shops shuttered. All the students had left the University of Dreams. The Dream Temples were deserted, shunned by the people of Beau Revere, who never wanted to have a dream ever again.

Rose looked around. Evening was falling over the deserted stalls. "Quiet, isn't it. Where is everyone?" Scrape made no reply. Rose tugged impatiently at his sleeve and repeated, "I said, where is everyone?"

"Sorry, I didn't catch what you said." The jester shrugged. "Many stay at home. If someone dozes off and the Knyghtmare comes for them, sometimes they start talking in their sleep. Then everybody knows what dreams they've had. It's bad enough when it happens in front of their own families, but if it happened in public..." Scrape shook his head. "We all have secrets; some so deep and dark that it would destroy us if they were to become known."

Rose said nothing but looked thoughtful.

Scrape beckoned and led them into a small shop at the side of the square. It had an awning outside and, unlike the neighbouring businesses, showed some signs of life.

They entered to a buzz of conversation. People – mostly men – were talking animatedly to each other. They were all drinking some kind of dark liquid from small cups.

The air was full of a rich, earthy aroma.

"Some people come to places like this for company,"

explained Scrape. "Talking passes the time, and coffee is supposed to help you stay awake."

Will looked blank. "Coffee?"

Scrape waved to a waiter, who brought over three of the tiny cups. "Don't you have coffee in your city?"

Rose sniffed at her cup and wrinkled her nose. Will took a sip of the astringent brew and burst out coughing. Eyes streaming, he shook his head. "I can see why they call it 'cough-ee'."

"It's an acquired taste, I suppose." Scrape sipped at his coffee with apparent enjoyment.

Will stared dubiously at the murky brown liquid in his cup. "Does it keep you awake?"

There was a disturbance in the corner behind them. A man, who had evidently fallen asleep despite the noise and the coffee, suddenly started up. Pawing at his clothes and screaming, "Begone demons! They plague me! Blue and hairy, aaarghh!" he staggered out of the shop.

Scrape gave Will a lugubrious smile. "Not always."

Rose was watching a man sitting near the door. He was rocking back and forth, giggling and crooning to himself. Rose nudged Scrape. "What happened to him?"

The jester shook his head sadly. "He was a shepherd." Will and Rose looked blank. Lowering his voice, Scrape said, "You know what happens when you count sheep." Understanding dawned. "Every time he counted them, he'd go out like a light," Scrape went on. "And every time he went to sleep, he'd dream one of his sheep was missing, so he'd wake up and count them, and he'd fall asleep, and dream one of them was missing, and he'd wake up and count them..." Scrape shook his head morosely. "Drove him mad in the end, poor chap."

"What will happen to him?" asked Rose.

"Somebody will feed him, if they remember," said Scrape. "It could be worse. When the Knyghtmare gets to them, some people try to run away. They rush off into the Forest beyond our walls, screaming their heads off, and they never come back."

Rose thought of some of the creatures that lived in the Dark Forest. "No," she said, suppressing a shudder, "they wouldn't."

Scrape finished his drink and led the way out of the shop. As they emerged into the square, the jester pointed at a robed figure hurrying towards them. His head was covered by an enormous bandage and he kept casting apprehensive glances upwards. "One of the Emir's counsellors," said Scrape. "He dreamt that a chimneypot was going to fall on his head and now he's just waiting for it to happen. He wears that bandage to save time when it does."

The man panted to a halt before them. "O jester," he gasped, "his Most Fanciful Highness the Emir is calling for you."

Scrape turned to Will and Rose and gave them a wry half-smile. "Hey ho, a jester's work is never done, with a snip-snap-snorum, high cockolorum, folderol, folderol-day." He cut a woebegone caper. "Pathetic isn't it?" He trailed off in the messenger's wake, forlornly hopping from foot to foot. Will and Rose stood and watched until he was out of sight and the tinkling of his bells had faded into silence.

From a nearby house came a scolding female voice: "No, you can't go to sleep. I want you out of those pyjamas this minute! I did not say your sister could go to sleep, and anyway, that's different, she's older than you. I don't care if Dolly wants to sleep, you have to stay awake. Because I say so, that's why. Oh, your friend Amme is allowed to go to sleep is she? And if your friend Amme was allowed to jump off a minaret, would you want to go and jump off one too? Don't you talk to your mother like that..." There was a slap and a shriek, and the voice faded to distant muttering.

In a troubled voice, Rose said, "Can dreaming really be that bad?"

"Try to remember some of your worst dreams," said Will.

Rose closed her eyes in concentration. "Oh dear," she said.

"And apart from the last few we had out in the Forest," said Will grimly, "you managed those dreams all by yourself. Just imagine what sort of dreams you'd have if they were being sent by somebody who really wanted you to suffer."

"I'm trying not to," said Rose. "Just don't let me fall asleep." She thought for a moment. "Let's say you're right about this Knyghtmare: that somebody must be behind it."

"Do you have any better ideas?"

Rose shook her head. "But if that's true, whoever is controlling it must have either brought it to the city or created it themselves."

"That makes sense."

"The sixty-four thousand groat question is 'who?'"

Will's eyes narrowed in concentration. "What would Humfrey do in this situation?"

"That's obvious – he'd make a list of suspects."

"Then that's what we'll do!" exclaimed Will. "So who's your chief suspect?"

"Shayde," said Rose without a second's hesitation.

Will grimaced. "You really don't like her, do you?"

"That doesn't enter into it," replied Rose loftily. "The person behind the Knyghtmare is probably someone pretty high up in the palace, and of all the people we've met, Shayde is the most likely. She must have been hopping mad at being made to marry that old grouch. I would be."

"Mad enough to drive lots of people you don't even know out of their minds with fear?" Will shook his head stubbornly. "I don't think so. There's no evidence that it's Shayde."

"And there's no evidence that it *isn't*," replied Rose.

Will ignored her. "If you ask me, it's probably the Vizier. He knows all about the world of dreams *and* he's really got it in for us."

"And that's *your* evidence?" said Rose pointedly.

Will gave a sigh. "Well, until we find out more facts, we have to suspect everyone." A thought popped into his head. "Even the Emir himself!"

Rose snorted. "Why should the Emir ruin his city by driving his own subjects insane? Talk sense! My money's still on Shayde."

Will realised that further discussion was going to get them nowhere. "There's only one way to find out. Come on." He set off across the twilit square.

Rose called after him, "And what's that? Where are you going?"

"To find a nice, soft bed. And a bath first, if I can get one."

"I thought you were going to try and save the city!"

"I am. And to do that, I have to go to sleep." Will made a wide gesture that took in the whole of Beau Revere. "We're not going to find the Knyghtmare here. This isn't where he lives. The only way we can find out who he is, is for me to find him and challenge him in his own world. In the dream world."

"You know shomething?" said Humfrey the Boggart reflectively. "Thish ishn't a bad way to travel once you get ushed to it."

"Glad you think so," said Tym shortly. He was used to travelling hundreds of leagues at wind speed with little or no rest, but not carrying a passenger. Even with Humfrey's moderate weight, he was beginning to tire. Sweat was dripping into his eyes, his legs were starting to feel wobbly, his shoulders ached and his breathing was becoming ragged. It was a good thing that darkness was falling: soon, it would be time to stop.

Humfrey, on the other hand, had grown used to their speed and was becoming talkative. "Yessir. Pretty relaxing. In fact, I'm shtarting to feel a little peckish. I wonder what Luigi packed for ush to eat."

"Pasta, I expect."

Humfrey groaned. "Pashta! That'sh no food for a growing boggart. What I wouldn't give for a haunch of venishon – or a young hare, jugged sho that it meltsh in your mouth..." He closed his eyes. "...or a nice plump chicken with shtuffing and bread shauce – or a..."

"Duck!" yelled Tym.

A beatific smile spread across Humfrey's homely face. "Exactly! A nice, juicy, crishpy roasht duck—"

An unexpected and stout horizontal branch, which Tym had lowered his shoulders to avoid, hit the hungry boggart smack in the face, lifting him bodily from Tym's shoulders and depositing him, deeply unconscious, in the leaf mould and dust of the Forest floor.

"You're not going to do this!" cried Rose. "You've seen what happens to people who go to sleep when the Knyghtmare is around. People are more scared of going to sleep than getting their heads chopped off!"

"Night-night." Will turned on his side and pulled the bed cover up to his chin.

Rose stormed round to the other side of the bed, which

was oval, with silken sheets and hangings in pastel shades and, in Rose's opinion, more pillows than was strictly necessary. On their return to the palace, Will had made his wishes known and an army of servants had led them to a suite of sumptuous rooms, providing Will with a strange form of nightwear that they called pyjamas. The servants were evidently under orders to grant the strangers every assistance in the hope that they could fulfil their promise to rid the city of the Knyghtmare. Until we fail, thought Rose grimly. After that, they'll probably send us to sleep in the dog kennels – if we're lucky.

She knelt beside the bed and rested her forearms on it so that she could shout into Will's face, "I shall poke you if you don't stop it." She jabbed a vicious finger into Will's ribcage. "Poke... poke... poke..."

Will opened his eyes. "Is there a problem?"

"Yes, there's a problem! I thought we were supposed to be finding the Knyghtmare together."

"Have you ever seen the Knyghtmare?" asked Will. Rose said nothing. After a few moments, her head gave a reluctant shake. "Well, I have. He showed himself to me. I'm sure it was meant as a challenge."

"You don't know that," said Rose fiercely.

"Not for certain, no – but then, we don't know anything for certain, do we?"

"Oh... you!" Rose jumped to her feet and paced up and down in front of the bed. "You twist everything to mean what you want it to mean, just to give you the excuse to do what you want to do. How do I know you'd even seen this black Knyght before your dream was read in the throne room? And then, the Knyghtmare wasn't challenging you, was it? It was challenging the Emir, if anything."

"You've got it all wrong."

"As usual," said Rose sarcastically, "you've decided that you're going to 'save the city' by defeating the Knyghtmare in single combat, which is as brainless an idea as I've ever heard, particularly as even you have to admit it probably doesn't even exist in the real world. So what am I supposed to do while you're snoring your stupid head off?"

"I don't snore!"

"Twiddle my thumbs? Or maybe you'd like me to embroider my initials on a scarf so you could wear it on your helmet, if you had one—"

"There's no need to shout."

"I am not shouting! And if I am, it's all your fault. You've just decided what you're going to do without even talking to me about it. Well, have it your way. Go to sleep, see if I care." Rose sat on the edge of the mattress with her arms folded, her legs crossed and a scowl on her face that would terrify a gargoyle.

Will protested, "Look, it really isn't like that." Rose gave no sign of listening, but he ploughed on, "It seems to me, we have two threats to watch out for." Rose stirred. "We know that the Knyghtmare controls dreams, but we think someone in the real world is controlling the Knyghtmare. Maybe, if I can defeat the Knyghtmare, I can find out who that is. But whether I can or not, while I'm in the dream world, I'll be asleep in the real world, so I'll be vulnerable to attack."

Rose turned to face him. "So what you're saying is that we make a two-pronged attack – you challenge the Knyghtmare in the dream world, while I try to find out who's behind it in the waking world?"

Will nodded encouragingly. "And anyway, I need you to watch me while I sleep, so you can wake me up if something goes wrong."

Rose glowered at him. "When you start going all reasonable on me, I know you're up to something—"

One of the palace servants burst into the room and bowed low. "O strangers," he said breathlessly, "your magical talking dulcimer..."

Will stared. "What?"

Rose rolled her eyes. "He means the Harp." To the servant, she said, "What's it done now?"

The servant's eyes were round with horror and delight. "It told Vizier Shaman al'Seer to 'go sit in an egg cup and hit himself over the head with a spoon'! The Vizier waxes wrathful."

"I bet he does," said Rose, trying not to giggle.

"He says the instrument is possessed of a jinnee, and he swears he will destroy it, but the Emir's daughter has taken it into her keeping and says she will not let him have it, and there is much discord."

Will sat up in bed. "Come on."

Rose pushed him back. "Leave this to me. You're not properly dressed. In any case, I don't think it's a good idea for you to get in the Vizier's way right now, and you've certainly seen quite enough of Shayde for one day. Don't do anything until I get back. All right?" Will nodded. Rose swept out.

Will sat still for a while, thinking about nothing. When several minutes had passed and Rose still hadn't returned, he went to the door and looked up and down the corridor. Behind him, in the bedroom, a shadow moved across the floor – and back again...

Will closed the chamber door and lay on the bed, propped up on one elbow. He reached for the flask of iced sherbet that a servant had left on the bedside table and poured himself a drink...

CHAPTER NINE

H ow Rose put her Rival in the Shayde, and
Will went to Sleep on the Job.

R ose found the Vizier hammering on the door to Shayde's
apartments, promising all sorts of dreadful consequences if
she didn't come out, while the Emir fidgeted and clucked
in the background like an anxious mother hen. Then, after
several minutes of clattering, threats and fearful oaths, it
emerged that Shayde wasn't in her rooms at all. She came
pacing demurely down the corridor towards the apoplectic
Vizier and told him matter-of-factly that she had put the
Harp in a safe place where he would not find it, adding in
a mock-concerned voice that he would burst a blood vessel
if he carried on like that.

The Vizier stormed off. The Emir mopped his face with a silk handkerchief the size of a bed sheet and begged his daughter not to provoke the worthy and enlightened Vizier. Couldn't she see what it did to his poor nerves? Eventually, he too wandered off, leaving Rose alone with Shayde.

To Rose's amazement, the Emir's daughter invited her into the royal apartments and called for refreshments. Shayde, reclining on a couch, observed Rose through hooded eyes and nibbled at tiny sugary confections with her pearly white teeth. Rose determined that, in response to this courtesy, she would be on her very best behaviour – and not, for instance, shake Shayde until she rattled, or lay her out with a straight left to the jaw.

After several uncomfortable minutes of sipping tea (which was quite different from the nettle tea Rose brewed at home – for one thing, it didn't leave her mouth feeling numb for a week), Rose said, "Thank you for the tea. May I have the Harp now, please?"

Shayde was watching Rose with cat-like calculation. She raised a delicate eyebrow and said, "First, O stranger girl, tell me this – are you enamoured of your companion?"

Rose gave her a killing glare. "Me? In love with Will? Certainly not. But then, neither are you. Come on, girls together. Admit it."

"You must not say such things to me. It is a great impertinence." A mischievous light glittered momentarily in Shayde's dark eyes. "I will buy him from you, if you have a prior claim. I am astonishingly wealthy."

Rose stared at her. "Now you're being silly. Will doesn't

belong to me, and we don't buy and sell people where we come from. Anyway, it doesn't change the fact that you don't care about him at all."

Shayde pouted. "He is my betrothed."

"Only if he manages to defeat the Knyghtmare," Rose reminded her. "In any case, you're only using him to annoy the Vizier. Have you thought about what you'll do if we really do manage to save the city?"

"I shall marry the stranger youth," Shayde replied haughtily, "and beguile him with sweetmeats and pomegranates. I shall shower upon him rich gifts of ivory, apes and peacocks."

"Oh, lovely. Just what he's always wanted!" Rose's exasperation threshold had never been very high. "Look, this is ridiculous. Why don't you just tell the Vizier you don't want to marry him?"

Shayde sat up, abandoning her languid attitude. "Insolence! And foolishness." Her eyes filled with hot, angry tears. "You have no understanding. I am the Emir's daughter – the heir to the throne – and I may not bestow my heart where I will. But I shall not marry Shaman. I hate him – hate him!"

For the first time, Rose felt a little sorry for Shayde, but she hardened her heart and said, "How much do you hate him? Enough to bring the Knyghtmare down upon the whole city just to give you an excuse to break off your betrothal?"

With a shriek of rage, Shayde flew at Rose, scratching and clawing. But despite her fury, she did not know how to fight at all. Rose sidestepped neatly, caught the young woman's wrists and threw her back on to the bed, face down, with her arms pinioned behind her back. Shayde struggled for a while, then gave way to passionate weeping.

Rose didn't know whether to hug Shayde or slap her. "Stop that!" Shayde's wails became louder. "Listen, if you want to marry Will..." To her disbelief, tears started in Rose's eyes. Furiously, she blinked them away and continued, "that's between the two of you. It's nothing to do with me." She let go of Shayde's arms and stood up. "Now, are you going to tell me where the Harp is?"

Shayde looked up at Rose with sulky, red eyes. "In the women's quarters," she said at last. "Men are not allowed there."

"Thank you." Rose turned to go.

Shayde sat up. "Have a care, O barbarian girl who fights like an alley cat!" Her mouth twisted into a bitter smile. "Perhaps I have some influence with the Knyghtmare. Perhaps I shall have him send you a dream that will make your bowels dissolve into water."

Rose gave Shayde her very sweetest smile. "Oh, I don't think so," she said amiably. "I have very strong bowels. Thank you for the tea."

Directed by a maidservant, Rose went to the women's quarters and collected the Harp ("Do you have to drag me away so soon? If these aren't the cutest concubines I've ever seen, call me a lyre...") before making her way back to Will's chamber.

"Shayde threatened to set the Knyghtmare on me," she announced, bursting in with her usual lack of ceremony. "Nice girlfriend you've got." She stood the Harp on an ornate dressing table and turned to face the bed. "I don't know whether she was talking big because I'd just given her a whupping, or..."

Her voice trailed off. Will was asleep.

Rose clenched her fists until her nails cut into her palms. How could he do this? They'd agreed! He'd promised! She turned on her heel.

"Hey!" cried the Harp. "Where do you think you're going?"

"To find my bow," snapped Rose, "and then a way out of this city."

"Running out on us, are you?"

"Me?" Rose jabbed a finger at Will's sleeping figure. "He's the one who's running out. He's gone to challenge the Knyghtmare in the dream world. He wasn't supposed to do anything until I came back. He promised! And look at him! Well, he can have Shayde if he wants her—"

"I hate to interrupt you while you're having a paranoid episode," drawled the Harp in its most offensive voice, "but what in the woods are you talking about?"

"Well, it's obvious why he's gone off to dreamland without me like this, isn't it?"

"Is it? It must be my day for failing to spot the obvious. Why do you think he's gone off without you?"

"To impress Shayde! If he beats the Knyghtmare, he gets to marry her! All I can say is, the best of luck to both of them and I hope it rains on their wedding day."

116

"Weeelll," said the Harp judiciously, "I daresay you're right about everything as usual. There's just one tiny thing that bothers me."

Rose paused with her hand on the door. "Yes?"

"How come Will hasn't woken up? You've been screeching around the place like a banshee's hen night. How's he managed to sleep through that?"

Rose felt a cold hand clutch at her heart. She threw the Harp an appalled glance, then hesitantly crossed the floor and approached the bed. Bending over the hunched shape beneath the bedclothes, she said softly, "Will?" Steeling herself, she shook the sleeping figure gently by the shoulder. "Will?"

The door flew open, almost tearing itself off its hinges, and the Vizier strode into the room.

"Where is he?" he roared. "Where is the barbarian dog who would rob me of my bride? Let him promise what he will, I shall flay his insolent hide—"

"Don't you ever bother to knock?" snapped the Harp. "Why don't you go boil your ugly head – four and a half minutes so your brains are nice and runny."

Rose spun round from the bed. Between the shock of finding that Will would not wake, and the Vizier's entrance, she found herself speechless.

The Vizier stared at the recumbent figure of his rival. "What is this?" he demanded. "What ails the boy?"

Rose pulled herself together. "I found him like this," she said in a shaking voice. "I can't wake him up."

The Vizier looked around. His eyes lighted on the flask

beside the bed and the empty glass that lay on the coverlet, almost within reach of Will's outstretched hand. He raised the flask to his nose and sniffed delicately.

"He has drunk a powerful sleeping draught," he said with professional detachment. He sniffed the glass and nodded. "Its taste would have been disguised by the sherbet."

"Can you wake him?" asked Rose.

The Vizier shook his head decisively. "It is beyond my skill – or that of any Dream Reader." He stood up and said with grim satisfaction, "It seems that the sentence I had planned for him, he has carried out by his own hand."

"Hey, omelette-for-brains!" rasped the Harp. "I'd never have told you to go boil your head if I'd realised you'd gone and done it already!" The Vizier took a threatening step towards the Harp. "Ask yourself," it continued, "would anybody in their right mind take that knockout juice after they'd heard what was going on around here?"

Rose said uncertainly, "He said he was going to challenge the Knyghtmare..."

"Oh, for pity's sake! OK, I know the kid's got the intellect of a penny whistle but he's not completely stupid. All he had to do was go to sleep, right? Then, if things got tough, he could wake up – pep talk, quick rub down, review of tactics, and try again later. This way, he's trapped. He can't afford to louse up. He gets one shot at the title and that's it. Does that make any sense to you?" The Harp glared from Rose to the Vizier and back again. "Well, does it?"

The Vizier replaced the flask and straightened up, smoothing his robes. "It matters little. Whether he took the draught knowingly or unknowingly, the result is the same. He is in a sleep that cannot be broken, at the mercy of the Knyghtmare."

Tonelessly, Rose said, "What will happen to him?"

"The Knyghtmare renders its victims prey to agonies of self-doubt." Rose nodded; Scrape had told them that much. "I have tried to read the dreams of those who fall prey to the Knyghtmare," Shaman continued, "but I was forced to desist. The experience was too painful." Rose looked sharply at the Vizier, and, to her astonishment, saw that his pride, aggressiveness and boundless self-confidence had fallen away like so many cloaks, leaving the man looking vulnerable and diminished. She suddenly realised that the Vizier was even older that she had first thought.

Shaman had been lost for a moment in his memories – obviously painful ones, for he continued, "To see the sufferings of those poor, helpless minds: no man could bear it." He shook himself. "At any rate, I was able to learn – or surmise – something of the Knyghtmare's mode of attack.

"The creature preys on its victims thus: it offers them moral choices. If they make the wrong choice, if they act from fear or self-interest, they have failed the Knyghtmare's test and are subject to the most vile and terrible visions. They are seized by despair; they run mad; eventually, death follows." The Vizier's face was skull-like in the dim lamplight. "The manner of death reflects the events of the dream."

"How?" asked Rose in a whisper.

"I can give you examples. You have had a dream where you suddenly felt yourself to be falling?" Rose nodded. "In the last, most severe stages of the Knyghtmare's sending, if you did not awake before the end of the fall, you would die. If you dreamt you were in a battle and wounded unto death, then you would die indeed. With no disease or injury, without a single mark on your body, you would die."

There was a heavy silence. Then the Harp said, "You seem to know a lot about this Knyghtmare character."

The Vizier gave the Harp a withering look. "I am Chief Dream Reader of Beau Revere. I would be failing in my duties if I did not."

The Harp considered for a moment. "OK, what you've said doesn't sound good, but if I read you right, all the kid has to do is make the right choice and he'll be fine. Am I right?"

"Would that it were so," said the Vizier solemnly. "Unfortunately, there is a catch."

The Harp gave a whistle of feigned astonishment. "You know what, I kinda guessed there might be. And that is...?"

"There is no right choice! In the cases I have examined, the victims were given two alternatives, either of which was disastrous! The Knyghtmare always put the worst possible interpretation on anything its victims decided, so that even an impulse to do good was twisted into one of cynical self-interest. And if the victim failed to choose at all, he or she fell prey to a paralysing agony of indecision and self-loathing. No matter what choice they make, or fail to make, they cannot escape the Knyghtmare."

Will twitched in his sleep. A spasm crossed his face, a momentary expression of what might have been pain – or fear...

"Can we find out what he's dreaming?" asked Rose hesitantly.

The Vizier bowed curtly. "I can have a crystal brought here and read your friend's dream—"

"No!" Rose's voice was sharp. She moved to stand between the Vizier and Will, fiercely protective. "I don't trust you. For all I know, you may have put the sleeping draught in Will's drink yourself."

The Vizier drew himself up proudly. "I was angry with the boy, that is true. He would steal my betrothed. But I would not act in such an underhand and dishonourable manner. I would have given the youth such a draught under the auspices of the law, but I am no assassin." Without a further glance at Rose or the Harp, he strode out of the room.

The Harp said, "I hate to say this, but you might have given ol' pebble-head's offer a little more thought..."

Rose rounded on him. "How could I? What I said was true. Shaman might have put that stuff in Will's drink."

"How? I thought he was with you at the time. In any case, why would he have come bursting in here to have a go at the kid if he knew he was asleep already?"

"He couldn't know for sure whether Will had drunk the potion. Anyway, it might be all a clever double bluff. And he wasn't with me all the time – only until Shayde appeared. They had a row and he stomped off. He could have come back here while I was with Shayde. So could the Emir."

"Right," the Harp mused. "But at least that puts Shayde in the clear."

"No it doesn't! Shaman was banging on her door for ages before she turned up. She could have come from anywhere."

"So she could have slipped Sleeping Beauty here the knockout drops before she met you, or the Vizier or the Emir could have done it afterwards?"

"Or any one of them could have ordered a servant to do it while they were miles away with a hundred witnesses! And I daren't go to sleep and try to help Will in the dream world, because he could be attacked again in the real world at any time, and so could I!" She gave the Harp a look of hopeless despair. "There's nothing I can do, and there's no one I can trust. No one!"

CHAPTER TEN

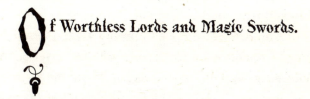

Of Worthless Lords and Magic Swords.

It was dark when Humfrey came to. He sat bolt upright and stared around wildly. *"Who did that? Shomebody get hish number! Call a doctor! Call my attorney!"* He gazed blankly for a moment at his surroundings, then put his hands to his head and groaned. *"I'm not here."*

"An unusual opening to a conversation," boomed the Dreamwalker's deep voice, *"but essentially correct. At this moment, your physical body is lying unconscious in the depths of the Dark Forest."*

Humfrey nodded dumbly. He found he was standing on the desolate plain of the Dreamwalker's country. As he turned to face the gigantic shadowy creature, the Dreamwalker gestured with one hand. A half-transparent image of Tym appeared, kneeling on the sandy ground. He was holding the stunned boggart by the front of his tunic and shaking him violently. *"Come on, Humfrey!"* The Whizzard's frantic voice seemed to come from a great distance. *"Wake up! We have to find Will and Rose. Come on!"* Tym slapped Humfrey on both cheeks.

"Hey, kid!" Humfrey was incensed at Tym's ill-treatment of his unresponsive body. *"Lay off the rough shtuff!"* He turned to the Dreamwalker. *"Tell him to can it! Doesn't he know you should never move shomebody who just head-butted a tree? What'sh more, he'sh gonna messh up my rugged good looksh."*

The Dreamwalker waved his hand again and the vision faded. *"Alas,"* he said, *"I cannot communicate with the Whizzard unless he is asleep, nor can I return you to a state of consciousness before your body has recovered from the blow it sustained. But do not be concerned; you will return to the waking world presently. Until then, it occurred to me that you might profit from some knowledge of the recent history of Beau Revere."*

Humfrey nodded. *"Makes shenshe. I'm not going to achieve anything jusht lying there in a shtate of unconshioushnessh."*

The Dreamwalker looked puzzled. *"I am sorry – I did not quite understand what you..."* Enlightenment dawned. *"Ah. Did you say, 'unconsciousness'?"*

"Sure I did," said Humfrey pugnaciously. *"Shay, d'you think I could have a chair here?"* The Dreamwalker gestured.

A comfortable winged-back armchair appeared. Humfrey gave it a disparaging look. *"That doeshn't really fit in with my image. Maybe shomething less shumptuoush?"*

The Dreamwalker looked puzzled but gestured again. A simple hardwood chair appeared. This time Humfrey gave a satisfied nod and sat on it the wrong way round, with his arms folded across its back. *"That'sh better. OK, big guy, shpill the beansh."*

The Dreamwalker was obviously not used to speaking Humfrey. *"Do you mean you wish me to begin?"*

"That'sh what I shaid."

"Very well." The Dreamwalker gestured again. The image of a tubby figure in silken robes and a turban appeared, hovering above the dusty plain, slowly revolving. *"This is Emir Raj, the present ruler of Beau Revere – at least he was still the ruler when I was last able to visit my city."* The Dreamwalker sighed. *"There is no harm in him, but he is not the most effective ruler in the city's history. Had destiny not decreed otherwise, he would not have been Emir at all."*

"How come?" demanded Humfrey.

"His predecessor, Emir Bagatelle, had a son." Two more figures appeared: a pale, stern-looking man in royal robes and a dark-haired youth who was tall, slim and well-made, but whose expression was full of ill-humour and malice. There was also something wrong... Humfrey was startled to realise that the Emir's son was missing an ear.

"Young Jasper was a great disappointment to the Emir. The boy was ungovernable: disobedient, cruel, ill-natured, tyrannical and vindictive." A series of images followed, of

Jasper bullying servants, stealing, beating a dog... *"That is how he lost his ear,"* continued the Dreamwalker. *"He ill-treated one of the Emir's hunting dogs and the poor beast turned on him. The dog was put down: there were many at the time who said that the Emir destroyed the wrong animal."*

Humfrey blanched at one particularly gruesome scene. *"I've heard of kidsh pulling the wingsh off flies... but pulling the wingsh off ducksh..."* He shuddered.

The Dreamwalker sighed. The images became small dust-devils that spun across the plain for a little way before collapsing. *"In an attempt to turn him from wickedness and folly and remind him of his duty, I sent the wretched youth one bad dream after another, each one worse than the one before, but to no avail. My Dream Readers also did their best to supply guidance, but in the end they were unable to turn the boy from his evil course. Furthermore, the most gifted seers at the University of Dreams all predicted he would one day bring disaster on the city. Recognising that all his subjects had turned against Jasper, the old Emir disinherited his worthless son on his deathbed, and passed the rule of Beau Revere to his cousin Raj."*

"What happened to the kid?"

The Dreamwalker gestured again and an image of the palace of Beau Revere appeared. It was night and the palace was on fire. Flames leapt, dense smoke billowed; minarets and towers toppled, roofs fell in, walls crumbled. *"The very night the old Emir died, the wing where he and his son lived was razed to the ground; no one got out alive. So Jasper perished and Raj came to the throne."* The Dreamwalker gestured again and the vision faded. *"Yet Emir Raj's position* is not altogether secure," it continued. *"Many of the nobles in the Emir's court felt that his predecessor's favour should have fallen on them."*

Once more, images formed in the desert air of a bald-headed, black-robed man whose eyes seemed to burn with an inner fire, and a raven-haired girl with a petulant mouth and hooded eyes. *"One such noble,"* the Dreamwalker continued, *"Shaman al'Seer, became Emir Raj's Grand Vizier. He rules the City in all but name, but is still subject to the whims of the Emir, and cannot forget that he might have been Emir himself had the election fallen more favourably. And the Emir's daughter, Shayde, would rebel against the destiny that condemns her to marry the Vizier when she comes of age – if she could find the means of doing so."*

"Thish shet-up ish loushy with motives," Humfrey observed thoughtfully. *"Shayde hash one, Shaman hash one, the Emir hash one..."*

The Dreamwalker was startled. *"The Emir? Surely not."*

"No? You shaid yourshelf, he'sh the short of guy nobody takes sherioushly. What if he'sh created the Knyghtmare to keep hish enemiesh too busy to plot againsht him? I've known shtranger... Hey!" Humfrey protested as the Dreamwalker's plain began to fade, *"What gives? We're not finished here! Why are you shending me away?"*

The Dreamwalker's voice faded as Humfrey felt himself falling with infinite slowness, away from the realm of dreams. *"I am not sending you away, Master Boggart. You are regaining consciousness. Remember what you have learnt – in Beau Revere, nothing is what it seems..."*

...And then the Dreamwalker's voice faded altogether and Humfrey awoke, lying on his back on the twiggy floor of the Dark Forest. The sun had set, but the boggart was aware of someone bending over him. Someone whose breath smelt like a slaughterhouse on a hot day. Humfrey coughed. "Hey, kid – did anyone ever tell you, you should pay more attention to dental hygiene?"

"I don't think so," came the response, "but thanks most awfully for the tip."

Humfrey froze. That wasn't Tym's voice. He opened his eyes and found himself staring into a set of very sharp and deadly fangs.

"Welllll, hellooooooooo..."

Will stood before the black Knyght.

The Knyght sat motionless. Its visor was down; nevertheless, it seemed to be watching Will closely. The pennant on its lance, the sable caparisons of its horse, snapped in the fresh breeze.

Will's mind raced. He must have fallen asleep – but he'd promised Rose not to do that! She was going to be seriously unhappy. What had made him...? Will groaned inwardly. The drink! Someone must have drugged him. He steeled himself. After all, he'd planned to confront the Knyghtmare anyway; he'd just rather have had the option of waking up if things went wrong...

"Boy," said the Knyghtmare in a voice that seemed to come from a great distance, "would'st challenge me?"

Will said quietly, "I would."

The Knyghtmare gave a bark of contemptuous laughter. "You are a hedge-knyght, a travel-stained vagabond, a mere ragamuffin."

Will looked down at his thin and battered breastplate, at the holes in his tarnished hauberk, at his notched sword. Raising his head, he said, "Nevertheless, I challenge you."

The horse reared and pawed at the sky. Keeping his seat with ease, the black Knyght cried, "So be it!"...

...and Will found himself in the Great Hall of the Castle of Dun Indewood. But not the moth-eaten, draughty hall he knew. The high windows were unbroken, the banners and tapestries were unfaded, the wooden rafters and stalls unblackened by age and soot. The hall was filled with the warm light of candles and torches, and in the middle of it, on a platform adorned with cloth-of-gold, a King lay dead.

Will shook himself. The Age of the Kings had been long ago. There had been no King in the City for hundreds of years. It seemed that the Knyghtmare's challenge had brought Will deep into Dun Indewood's past.

The King, in his royal robes with his crown beside his head, was surrounded by solemn-faced courtiers, finely dressed, their faces sorrowful. At the head of the mourners stood an old man with a long white beard. With a thrill of shock, Will recognised the Runemaster. And standing on the old man's right was a hulking, scowling, mean-looking youth. Will stifled a gasp. Symon Mandrake!

Symon had been the bane of Will's young life growing up in Dun Indewood. For one thing, he had been Symon's whipping boy, which meant that whenever Symon did wrong, Will was punished. As Symon loved seeing Will punished, he made sure that he did wrong pretty much all the time. Symon had also been the High Lord Gordin's heir, and as such, Will (along with everyone else in Dun Indewood) had to do what Symon told him.

But Symon had been exiled when his father was defeated in the struggle for the Dragonsbane. It was thought that he had fallen prey to one of the many dangers of the Dark Forest. So what was he doing here?

Will shook his head, reminding himself that he was asleep. This was just a dream, it didn't have to make sense. Dreams could mix past and present, and possibly the future. At that point in his musings, he received his third shock. The girl standing beside Symon – although she was dressed in Dun Indewood fashion rather than the loose-fitting trousers and bodice of Beau Revere – was undoubtedly Shayde.

Will's mind was buzzing. The key characters in the scene were people he knew, but the situation looked strangely like an illustration from one of the books of Knyghtly valour that he had avidly pored over while waiting to be punished for Symon's misdeeds.

Before Will had time to ponder further, the Runemaster spoke.

"The King is dead," he said heavily, "but when shall we say, 'Long Live the King'? Our beloved lord, old King

Anthracite, left no heir. Therefore, the better to preserve the peace of the realm and avert the prospect of civil war between rivals for the throne, I decree that a great tournament be held on New Year's Day; then, we shall decide who is to be our new King."

As the final words echoed in Will's mind, the hall faded – to be replaced by a cobbled street. Will found he was riding a donkey so small that his feet brushed the ground. Around him, finely dressed citizens thronged the narrow way, heading for one of the City gates. Flags and banners hung from the houses and shops that crowded in on either side. Will realised that he was riding through The Grumbles – in his day, the seediest and most dangerous of Dun Indewood's low-rent districts. In this time it was clean, well-kept and prosperous-looking.

It dawned on Will that Symon was riding ahead of him, mounted upon a high-stepping destrier – a warhorse. He was wearing golden armour and looking hot and frightened. Will was carrying Symon's helm and shield at his saddlebow. He was obviously acting as Symon's squire – as he had once before, in the real world.

After they had gone a few paces, Symon felt for the sword that should have been hanging at his side. Clapping his hand to his head in a theatrical demonstration of dismay, he cried, "Woe! Alack! I have left my sword at my lodgings, I find. Alas, it is impossible that I should compete in the tourney!"

Will, who knew that Symon had developed cowardice and evasion to a fine art, was instantly convinced that Symon had left his sword behind deliberately to avoid having to fight in the tournament. He grinned inwardly. Symon wasn't going to get away with this if Will had anything to do with it. He spurred forward and cried, "Fear not, sir Knyght! I will bring your sword."

Symon gave him a basilisk stare. "Thank you, good squire," he said through gritted teeth, "but I fear that cannot be. I remember me now that I did give all the people of the lodging free tickets for the jousts. So," he went on with heavy emphasis, "it is impossible that there should be anyone at home! Lackaday," he added for good measure.

"Fear not, my Lord," said Will, grinning nastily at Symon to show that he knew exactly what he was up to. He wheeled his donkey – and almost ran into Shayde, who was riding a pace or two behind him on a palfrey.

Will reined in and bowed his head in apology, but Shayde only said, "I will go with you."

In the blink of an eye, the crowds vanished and Will found himself with Shayde, standing in Dun Indewood's main square, Cloth Yard.

"Lo!" declaimed Shayde.

Will looked downwards at the ground. "What is?"

"Not 'low'! 'Lo'! as in 'behold'!" She pointed.

In the centre of the square there lay a massive stone, on top of which stood a huge anvil. And pinning the anvil to the stone was a great sword, whose hilts gleamed in the sunlight.

Will dismounted and went towards the stone, wondering.

As he got closer, he saw that there were words carved on the stone. They said:

Whoso pulleth out this sword of this stone and anvil
Is rightwise King born of the Dark Forest.

There was something strangely familiar about the scene, but before Will could work out why, Shayde, came up behind him and said, "See? Here is a fine sword for your master. Do you take it."

Staring at the sword, transfixed, Will shook his head.

"Take it," said Shayde again. "Take it and give it to your Lord, who will reward you richly. Or," she lowered her voice and in hushed, conspiratorial tones, said, "take it for yourself and become King in his stead."

Will hesitated, but his thoughts were racing. Dimly he became aware that he was no longer in the square, but in a vast open space under a sunless sky, surrounded by a multitude of silent watchers. Will glanced around. All that vast host was waiting for him to decide; waiting to see what he would do.

Still, Will hesitated. This was a glorious sword and obviously a thing of great power. It was far too rich and rare a weapon even to be touched by a lowly squire. What if Will tried to draw it from the stone and failed?

But on the other hand, how could he refuse the adventure? If fate had led him here and he turned away, would the silent watchers not despise him for his cowardice?

And if he took the sword, what then? Symon was his

Lord: he owed allegiance to him. Supposing he gave the sword to Symon, as his vows required? Symon would undoubtedly claim the kingship, even though he had not pulled the sword from the stone himself. And Symon was cruel, mean, spiteful, vengeful and stupid. He would make a terrible King.

Or should Will, knowing that he would make a far better King than Symon, keep the sword. Perhaps that was the object of his quest. If he became King, perhaps he could defeat the Knyghtmare. Will stared hungrily at the sword.

In his ear, Shayde whispered again, "Take it."

Will drew a deep breath, nodded and reached out for the sword.

CHAPTER ELEVEN

How Humfrey put a Wolf in a Hold, and Will hammered out a Solution.

The Harp watched with an uncharacteristically worried expression as Will twitched and mumbled in his sleep. "Looks like he's having a bad time of it in there."

Rose bit her lip. "I know," she said angrily, "but what can I do? If he was being attacked in the real world, I'd be at his side like a shot. But he's living in the dream world, and I'm stuck here twiddling my thumbs!" She kicked out savagely at a cushion, which sailed across the room shedding feathers as it flew.

The Harp was watching her apprehensively. "Hey, don't smash up the joint, I'm sure help is on the way from somewhere..."

"Where?" demanded Rose bitterly. "If this so-called Dreamwalker could do anything about the Knyghtmare, we wouldn't be in this mess in the first place, and nobody from Dun Indewood knows we're here. There's no help on the way from anywhere!"

"You're right," said the Harp morosely. "We're doomed."

Rose stared at it, "I thought you were supposed to be making me feel better! I'd just like you to know that you're doing a really terrible job!"

The Harp bristled. "Yeah, well, I don't do 'making people feel better'. On the other hand, I'm the Forest's leading expert on 'making people feel worse'. Everyone has his speciality."

Will twitched again. Rose kicked another cushion. "I'd try to get to sleep, to see if I could help him in the dream world – but until we know who's behind the Knyghtmare, I daren't do that."

"Yeah," said the Harp. "You can't help the kid if you've been murdered in your bed. Stands to reason." It was silent for a moment. "Look, maybe you should call old Dome-head back and—"

"No."

"OK, maybe you should ask Shayde to come here and—"

"No!"

"Have it your way, but you can't do this on your own. You can't keep watching over the kid for ever."

"Then I'll just have to watch him for as long as I can. And you can help by keeping me awake."

"Oh boy! Oh boy! Oh boy!" The Harp gazed up at Rose, its eyes sparkling with unholy glee. "Can I really?"

As Will's hand crept out, he suddenly remembered where he had seen a sword in a stone before. It had been another illustration from the book of Knyghtly lore. And he remembered the story that had gone with the pictures – the tale of a boy-King, royally born but raised in obscurity, who had proved his claim to the throne by drawing a magic sword from a stone.

The boy in the story had been the true-born son of the King. But Will wasn't the son of a King or anyone else highborn. He was the son of Edwid the Swineherd, who was not only as lowborn as you could get, but also, frankly, extremely smelly and a bit dim.

But then Will's expression hardened. So what? he thought. Why should I have to be nobly born to claim the sword? It's what I do that matters, not who my parents were. He reached for the sword again.

At that moment, Symon suddenly materialised before Will. In imperious tones, he cried, "Bring me the sword!"

"No, Will!" insisted Shayde. "Take the sword for yourself."

Will took the hilt of the sword in both hands. A look of exultation spread across his face. If only Rose could see him now!

And thinking of Rose, he paused. He imagined seeing Rose after he was made King, and showing her his sword and crown. And he knew exactly what she would say.

She'd say, "You took a what from a what? And would you mind explaining how that makes you King, exactly?"

Will took his hands from the sword, and straightened. "I will not."

Symon clenched his fists and gave a roar of fury. Shayde burst into peals of mocking laughter.

And suddenly the Knyghtmare was before him.

The black Knyght sat astride the black horse, lance raised, ready to charge. Behind him rode a thousand Knyghts in full battle armour.

In a terrible voice, the Knyghtmare said, "Take the sword."

Will repeated, "I will not."

The Knyghtmare gave a bark of savage laughter. "You have no choice. It is the only weapon you have to hand. Use it, or we shall slay you in your blood."

For a third time, Will said, "I will not."

With a howl of fury, the black Knyght lowered his lance, signalling the charge. A thousand Knyghts, armed to the teeth, spurred towards Will as the Knyghtmare cried, "Defend thee, Squire, or thou art but a dead man!"

Humfrey grimaced in the darkness. The creature looming over him was the no-good Highwaywolf who used to hang around Dun Indewood. "What are *you* doing here?" the boggart demanded.

"Well, d'you know," the wolf said languidly, "I felt the City was rather cramping my style; what with girls with crossbows, Whizzards who didn't have the decency to stand still and be eaten, uppity thieves – not to mention wish hounds and trolls..." It shuddered. "So I went to a dentist who made me this rather marvellous set of false fangs." The wolf grinned and its steel teeth sparkled in the light of the rising moon. "He did an excellent job, though I'm afraid, once he'd fitted them, it turned out to be a rather unwise career move." The wolf licked its chops in a significant way. "Anyway, I thought I'd try my luck in a – how shall I put it? – less urban setting, so here I am." The wolf growled deep in its chest. "And here you are. Isn't that lucky?" It winked at Humfrey. "For me, not for you, obviously."

"And where'sh the kid?"

The wolf grinned. "Wouldn't you like to know. Now, that's enough... ahem, *small* talk..." The wolf, chuckling at its own wit, completely failed to notice the glint in Humfrey's eyes. "It's time for the old *into the mouth and through the gums; look out, tummy, here it comes...*" Slavering jaws agape, the wolf lunged.

After several confused seconds, silence once again descended on the Forest. Dust and leaf mould began to settle. The moon disappeared behind a cloud.

A plaintive voice said, "Er... hello?"

"Yesh?"

"Do you *have* to sit on my spine?"

"Sure I do. How could I tie your back legsh together

with your tail if I didn't?" replied Humfrey, knotting away busily.

The Highwaywolf's somewhat strained voice replied, "Good point."

Silence. Then:

"I don't suppose I could prevail upon you to overlook our little *contretemps*?"

"You mean, let bygones be bygones?"

"Yes?"

"Nope."

"Not even if I said I was sorry? Really, really sorry?"

"Really, really, *really* shorry?"

"Yes!"

"Well, lemme shee... hmmmmmmmmmmm... nope."

"I hate you."

"I can live with it." Humfrey stood up and dusted his hands just as Tym raced into the clearing. The Whizzard screeched to a halt and hurled a bucket of ice-cold water all over the boggart.

Into the dripping silence, Tym said, half apologetically, half accusingly, "I thought you were unconscious."

"Ish that right?"

"I went to look for help. I found an abandoned village with an old well."

"Good for you." Humfrey turned to the wolf. "Did I hear a shnigger out of you?"

The wolf shook its head. "Not so much as a titter."

"Good."

Tym hung his head. "Sorry."

140

Humfrey sighed. "Forget it." He shook water from his eyes. "Come on, we'd better get going. Will and Roshe could be in real trouble by now..."

The Knyghtmare gave a roar of savage laughter. "Draw the sword and defend yourself, beggar-Knyght, and be false to your vows – or stay your hand and be chopped to pieces."

Symon guffawed. "Choose, knave. Live a traitor, or die a pig boy!" Shayde gave another mocking peal of laughter. The charging Knyghts lowered their lances as they thundered towards Will, every last one intent on spitting him where he stood.

Will's stunned brain finally began to function. The choice he was being offered was no choice at all: if he took the sword or if he rejected it, either way he would lose...

But was there another way? This was the dream world – why did he have to accept the situation that the Knyghtmare had created? Couldn't he change it?

Will held out his hands as if he were grasping something heavy. Slowly and deliberately he said, "Sledgehammer."

Instantly, he found himself holding a huge hammer with a solid iron head. The weight was so enormous and so surprising that he almost dropped it. Steadying himself and summoning up every ounce of his strength, Will swung the implement as hard as he could.

The hammer head slammed into the stone, smashing it to smithereens. The anvil gave out a single anguished note and shattered into dull grey shards. The sword fell free.

Symon and Shayde stopped laughing. The charging Knyghts reined in, their horses neighing and back-pedalling frantically in a cloud of dust.

Will grasped the sword. He had neither pulled it from the stone, nor left it there. But now he had it, and could use it. Raising the sword, he leapt at his adversary and brought the shining blade round in a glittering arc aimed to cleave the black Knyght in two. There was a deafening thunderclap and an eye-searing blast of light. When Will could see again, the Knyghtmare was gone, as were Symon and Shayde and the sword.

The silent watchers had moved forward to surround Will. Their faces were masks of anguish, sorrow, terror. The Runemaster stepped forward from their ranks. In a hopeless voice, he said, "You have doomed us all. The sword would have chosen our rightful King. Without it, there will be civil war as every nobleman fights for the mastery: misery, butchery, despair..." The old man gazed distractedly at Will, fierce accusation in his eyes. "Without the Sword, how can we choose whom we should follow? How? Tell me that!"

In a perfectly level voice, Will said, "As best you can. As everyone must."

And then Will was alone, facing the black Knyght who was sitting quietly on its horse, its trappings fluttering in the breeze.

The Knyghtmare said, mockingly, "Do you imagine that you have won?"

Will said nothing.

"You have won nothing, boy, except a very little more time."

I know, thought Will. But time is precious. If I can buy some time, distract the Knyghtmare, Rose may discover who's behind all this. And the sleeping potion has to wear off sometime. I must go through with this quest, and I must not fail.

The Knyghtmare seemed to read his thoughts. "But you *will* fail. Do not delude yourself. You have passed the first test, but that is only the beginning. Your reward for having survived it shall be to face another, more difficult test – then another, and another. Sooner or later, ultimately and inevitably, you will succumb. And when you do..." The horse snorted and pawed the ground; the Knyghtmare's voice grated with implacable menace. "When you do, you will be mine. For ever."

Rose looked up from her anxious vigil. "He seems to be sleeping more calmly now."

For several minutes, Will had been twisting, writhing, muttering and crying out in his sleep. Beads of cold sweat still stood out on his forehead, but his breathing had eased and his face had lost the pallid, agonised look that had accompanied the worst moments of an ordeal that Rose could only guess at. All she could tell was that some kind of crisis had passed.

"Yeah," said the Harp, "so maybe you could let go his hand now."

Rose hurriedly snatched her hand away from Will's. "I wish we knew what was happening to him."

"Well, at the risk of repeating myself," said the Harp, "the only way you can do that is to get ol' Dome-head in here so we can see what he's dreaming. That way, we might even get a few clues about who's behind this thing."

"No," said Rose stubbornly, and yawned. It was almost dawn. She was very tired. Despite herself, her shoulders sagged and her head hung lower and lower as sleep began to overcome her...

"Thank you, thank you, ladies and gentlemen!" cried the Harp in ringing tones. With a startled cry, Rose shot bolt upright. The Harp strummed a jaunty intro and announced, "I shall now continue my rendition of *Hits from the Holly Wood Musicals* with a selection of songs from *My Fair Damsel*, *Oaklahoma* and *Quest Side Story*..."

Rose groaned. "You're loving this, aren't you?"

"You said keep you awake, I'm keeping you awake. All together now...

> *"Ooooooooooooooooo – OAK lahoma*
> *Where the wind comes whistling through the trees,*
> *Where it numbs your toes, and chaps your nose,*
> *And it blows the hair right off your knees...!"*

Rose put her fingers in her ears. "I can't take much more of this."

The Harp broke off. "Whadda ya mean? We've got another fifty-three shows to go... and then we can start on the folk songs!"

Chapter Twelve

How a Mad Dog refused a Boon, and how Humfrey came in and the Emir went Out.

"Hey, you! Yes, you!"

Will blinked. Once again, he was standing in the Great Hall of the Castle of Dun Indewood. This time he had a huge tray of steaming pies precariously balanced on his shoulder. A harassed-looking serving man carrying a pile of empty platters was glaring at him. "Stop dawdling! There are people waiting to be served. Get to work!"

Will peered over the pies. Before him, sitting at a long rectangular table, was a host of Knyghts. But not exactly the Knyghts of legend. They didn't look like battle-hardened warriors: most were seriously overweight, with ruddy faces, bad posture and food stains down their tunics. Many were asleep. Others lounged with their feet up, digging dirt from under their fingernails with the points of their daggers.

Will stepped forward, only to stop dead in shock as he saw the figure at the head of the table. On a gilded wooden throne sat Sir Regynild le Bêtenoire (otherwise known as Mad Dog Reggie) the Headmaster of Dun Indewood's Knyght School. He was wearing a crown. Will gaped. The Knyghtmare had made Mad Dog a King? Well, the bad tempered, arrogant old brute had always ordered people about and made their lives miserable as if he were royalty anyway.

Evidently the second quest had begun. Once again, the Knyghtmare was reaching into Will's memories and distorting time, place, people and reality to serve its own ends. Will wondered what this next dream would be about. He shrugged, almost dislodging the pies. There was nothing for it but to play along and see what happened.

Mad Dog glared across the table at Will. "What are you about, you wool-gathering worm? There are hungry Knyghts at this table! Dish those pies out forthwith, before you find yourself among their ingredients!" Will stepped forward, balancing the pies carefully, to deliver them to the table. Moments later, he tripped over some obstruction on the floor. He made a despairing grab at the tray, but without success. Pies flew across the table as though shot from siege-engines. Will stood for a moment, stock-still with horror, as the faces of the Knyghts (many of them now dripping gravy, pastry and unidentifiable lumps of gristle) swivelled to fix him with furious stares.

A low chuckle sounded to his left. Will looked down – and saw that sitting just behind him, on one of the benches that ran down three sides of the table, was a Knyght in black armour. Of all the company, he alone wore a helm, with the visor down. And his right leg, stretched out before him, was the obstruction over which Will had tripped. Will gritted his teeth. The Knyghtmare had succeeded in making a fool of him before the whole company.

Sir Regynild, who had miraculously managed to avoid the pies, glared at Will. "How now, Sir Butterfingers," he said in his usual creaky, sarcastic voice. "Had I wanted a juggler, I'd have sent for one." The assembled Knyghts, toadying like anything, laughed heartily at this feeble witticism. The ones who had suffered most from the deluge of pies laughed loudest of all, but the looks they shot Will were far from amused.

Sir Regynild slammed his fist down on the table and the laughter stopped instantly. Knuckles clenched on the scarred wood, he gave Will a look of pure malice. "What do you mean by it, you vicious, verminous villain?" he demanded. "What d'you mean, you mumping, malodorous mooncalf, by bursting into my hall like a bolt from the bally blue and peltin' these poor perishin' people with putrid pies? What's yer name, you nauseating, no-account numbskull?"

Biting his lip with fury at the ease with which the Knyghtmare had made him look foolish, Will said, "Squire Willum de Sanglier, if you please, Sire."

Mad Dog Reggie gave a roar of outrage. "Whaaaat? You dare style yourself 'squire' when as anyone can see, y're no more than a sneaking, stinking, slobbering scullion?" All around the table, Knyghts shook their fists, swore horrible oaths and jeered at Will. "Guards!" Sir Regynild's voice rose above the babble. "Drag this jumped-up jackanapes off to jail and whip him into a jelly!"

But before the guards could seize Will, a ragged fanfare sounded from outside the Hall. All eyes turned to the great doors, which creaked open. A page in an ill-fitting tabard flounced in with an air of great self-importance, crying, "Sire! A damsel seeks audience with Your Highness."

"Does she, now?" Sir Regynild's furious scowl was transformed into a complacent leer. "A *helpless* damsel, I presume?"

The page bowed. "Yes, Sire."

"And pretty?"

The page smirked. "Oh, yes, Sire!"

"Then by all means, let her approach."

Will felt he was beginning to get used to the way the dream world operated, so he was hardly surprised at all to see that the damsel who entered the hall with a flourish and a curtsey to the assembled Knyghts, was Shayde. She was wearing a flowing, high-waisted dress, and a hat so tall and pointed that it brushed the cobwebs which hung in dusty festoons between the chandeliers. The Knyghts hurriedly straightened themselves up with a lot of 'hum-hawing', adjusting of armour, and furtive brushing of hair and smoothing of moustaches.

Shayde, her dark hair shining, was obviously aware of the impression she was making. She advanced to the foot of the table (where the youngest and lowliest of the Knyghts fell over themselves to make room) and cried, "My liege! I crave a boon!"

Sir Regynild eyed her with a lazy half-smile. "Crave away, m'dear," he purred. "Boons are my business."

"Sire," said Shayde, fluttering her eyelashes in a way that would have sent Rose into a fury, "my mistress has been captured by a terrible fire-breathing dragon!" At this point, there was a lot of shuffling and coughing. "I beg you to send one of these brave, valiant Knyghts to slay the worm and be her rescuer!"

There was an awkward silence while she tried in vain to get one of the brave, valiant Knyghts to meet her eye.

Sir Regynild coughed awkwardly. "Well, of course, anything for a lady – though fire-breathing dragons, I must say... damn dangerous, devious, dastardly devils, the lot of them." He looked around at his Knyghts. "Well? What about it? Any of you fellers fancy the job?"

There was more shuffling. The Knyghts shifted uneasily in their seats, looking everywhere but at Shayde or Sir Regynild. Will seethed. This was just like the Dun Indewood of his youth, where the Knyghts delighted in status and empty ceremony and never actually did anything. Without considering the wisdom of his action, he raised his voice and cried, "Sire, grant me this quest! I will undertake to fight the dragon and rescue the Lady!"

From the ensuing silence emerged what sounded like a

series of small thunderclaps. Startled, Will looked round – and realised that the sound was made by the Knyghtmare, beating its mailed hands together in slow, mocking applause.

Then pandemonium broke out. The hall resounded to the jeers and ill-natured guffaws of Knyghts who, while they were scared of undertaking the quest themselves, had no reservations about mocking someone who was willing to do so, provided he couldn't answer back.

Mad Dog, however, seized on this opportunity to save face. "Well done, that man," he said, with an ironic wink at his cronies who haw-hawed all the louder. "Off you go, have a nice quest and do be careful. They say dragons are hot stuff." The Knyghts fell about, roaring with mirth at their lord's wit.

Shayde was horrified at Will's offer. She looked him up and down with paralysing disdain. In a voice that dripped scorn, she said, "But my liege, he is a mere servant; a mean, contemptible, base-born slave." Will glared at her. He was beginning to think that Rose had a point about this girl. "Surely," Shayde went on, "you would not insult my mistress by sending this churl to be her rescuer."

Sir Regynild took a negligent swig at his goblet of wine. "I agree with your assessment entirely," he said, "but there you are, I'm afraid. He may not be much, but it's him or nothing."

Her face flushed with anger, Shayde swung to face Will. "Then it shall be nothing," she said in tones of withering scorn. "Slave, be not so hardy as to follow me." Eyes flashing, she bowed curtly to Mad Dog. "I shall tell my mistress that no help is to be had from the Court of Dun Indewood."

"You do that," said Sir Regynild, quite unmoved. "Thank you for calling. Do show yourself out. Close the door when you leave."

Shayde stuck her nose in the air and marched defiantly out of the hall, accompanied by some ill-natured catcalls from the Knyghts (though a few of the younger ones had the grace to look ashamed), while the Knyghtmare held Will's gaze with a singularly knowing and mocking look.

Suddenly, the Great Hall vanished and Will found himself in the stable yard with his sword at his side. He was standing next to a donkey identical to the one on which he'd ridden through Dun Indewood on his first quest. The donkey looked up expectantly. With a sigh, Will took a rope bridle from a peg in the wall and patted the animal's dusty neck. "I wonder where this challenge is going," he muttered to himself. "I hope I'm doing the right thing..."

"Eeeee-ooooorrrr," opined the donkey.

Moments later, Will rode awkwardly across the drawbridge of the Castle, his feet again brushing the ground as the willing donkey trotted down the hill and through the dark streets of Dun Indewood in pursuit of Shayde.

Back in the real world of Beau Revere, the Harp's voice continued to echo throughout the palace's marbled passages.

"Callous behaviour and cruelty to kittens,
Shortly resulting in warm furry mittens..."

Scrape poked his head around the door to Will's room. His bells jangled mournfully. "How is he?" he asked, raising his voice to be heard over the Harp's insistent strumming.

The Harp gave him an unfriendly look. "Hey, laughing-boy, d'you mind not interrupting? I've just sung li'l Miss Sleepy Head here the hit songs from seventy-four shows, and I'm going for the big finish." It strummed harder and bellowed,

"Wisecracks and insults and being outrageous,
Singing rude songs and annoying the neighbours;
Loud screeching voices and badly tuned strings,
These are a few of my favourite thiiiiiings!"

Rose, her eyes red and hollow from exhaustion, hurled a pillow at the Harp. It uttered a startled, unmusical squawk and fell to the floor with a discordant jangle. "Philistine," it muttered.

Into the ensuing silence, Scrape said glumly, "You have a visitor."

Rose's head snapped up. "I have a what?"

"Visitor. Quite a small one. I didn't catch the name, but he doesn't talk like the rest of ush... I mean us. Inquisitive little chap, too. He asked me all sorts of questions about who I was and how I got here." Scrape wriggled uncomfortably. "He was quite personal."

"He would be – he's a private inquestigator." Her tiredness forgotten and suddenly almost cheerful, Rose made a dash for the door. A moment later, she stuck her head back round it. "Stay with him," she told Scrape, nodding at Will. "All right?"

Scrape looked nonplussed, but nodded. "All right."

Rose disappeared. Moments later, she was back again. "And call me if he wakes up. Or if anything else happens. And don't let anybody in here. Especially Shayde. All right?" She paused before adding, "And Shaman and the Emir."

Scrape said, "All ri..." but realised that Rose had gone.

The jester sat on the edge of the bed watching Will, while holding a silent discussion about the patient's condition with his head-on-a-stick.

After a while, the Harp said, "Would you like me to sing?"

"Would you like me to tell a joke?"

"Fair enough."

Silence descended. Will slept on. Presently, he began to mutter and twitch again.

Rose burst into the audience chamber. "Humfrey!" She pounced on the startled boggart, gave him a rib-cracking hug and swung him in a complete circle. Humfrey's face was brick-red by the time she released him.

"Shay, shishter," he whispered, "I'm pleased to shee you, too, but go eashy on the welcome, willya?" He looked uneasily round at the courtiers who were watching the reunion, giggling and whispering behind their hands, and the Vizier, who stared icily back. "It'sh kinda unbecoming to a feller'sh dignity to be shwung around like a shack," the boggart continued, "you know what I mean?" Rose apologised profusely, then rather spoilt the effect by kissing Humfrey on the top of his head, which made him go redder than ever.

He turned to the Vizier. "Yeah, well, like I wash shaying, my rates are sheventy-five florinsh a day, plush exshpenshesh..."

"Expenses," translated Rose seeing Shaman's blank look.

"I *shaid* exshpenshesh," hissed Humfrey. He darted forward and picked at the silver pattern on the Vizier's black robes. "You got a thread comin' looshe there," he muttered. "Let me fix that for ya..." He pulled a needle from his lapel.

The Vizier, unused to the boggart's compulsive tidiness, snatched his hem out of Humfrey's grasp. "Let us understand each other," he said frostily.

"Good idea," agreed Humfrey. "I'll need a free hand, full co-operation, and nobody leaves town. OK?"

Holding his temper with difficulty, the Vizier said, "You claim the Dreamwalker sent you…"

"To find out who'sh behind the Knyghtmare and put them on ice. Yeah, that'sh about the shize of it."

"And how," demanded the Vizier, "can we be sure that you are not a mere impostor?"

"The Dreamwalker shaid," Humfrey remarked casually, "that you might be difficult and jusht in cashe, he told me about a dream you had." He winked at the Vizier, who had turned an interesting colour. "Naughty, naughty!" He turned to the members of the court who were standing around enjoying the show and raised his voice. "It sheemsh…"

With all the dignity he could muster, the Vizier said, hastily, "I withdraw my objection."

"Then let'sh get shtarted." Humfrey pointed at the Vizier. "You come with me, and bring one of thoshe globe watchamacallitsh."

The Vizier stiffened. "I do not take orders from a…" he sniffed, and said, as if the word had a nasty taste, "boggart."

Humfrey grinned at him. "If it helpsh, think of it as a compulshory requesht."

As the Vizier stalked away to find a dream viewer, Rose dragged Humfrey to one side. She gazed at the boggart with something approaching awe. "How do you know what Shaman's dreams are?"

"I don't," said Humfrey cheerfully. "Not a clue."

Rose was thunderstruck. "Then what…?"

"Bluffed it, kid. It'sh like shending a message to some big shot sayin', 'Fly! All ish dishcovered!' And whaddaya know, next thing you hear they're livin' shomewhere you never heard of under an asshumed name an' falsh whishkersh. All you gotta do ish hint you know shomething and let their conscience do the rest."

"Sneaky," approved Rose. "So how did you get here?"

"Tym brought me."

"Whizzard Tym?"

"Shhhh!" Humfrey put a stubby finger to his lips. "He had to go shtraight off again to report to the Dreamwalker."

"How much do you know about what's going on here?"

"Pretty much everything apart from what you two have been doing shince you arrived."

Rose gave Humfrey an outline of all that had happened since she and Will had found themselves in Beau Revere. The Boggart listened intently.

"Sho you left Will with Shcrape – thish jeshter guy?" he said.

Rose nodded. "He's a bit of an irritating wimp, but he seems harmless enough."

"Hmmmmm." Humfrey rubbed the sides of his mouth in concentration. "My first thought was to get Shaman to dream-read all the shushpectsh, but from everything you tell me, we'd be better off using him to find out what Will'sh dreaming."

"Are you sure?" Rose looked over her shoulder. The Vizier had returned and was waiting impatiently for the whispered conference to end. "I don't trust him."

"Neither do I, but it should be shafe enough. One of ush will be watching him and Will can't be any more at the mercy of the Knyghtmare than he ish now..."

Humfrey was interrupted by a grief-stricken wail that echoed around the chamber. Shayde burst in. Her languid manner had completely disappeared, her hair was awry, her eyes were wide and filled with tears. She came to an unsteady halt in the midst of the stunned courtiers and her voice cracked as she spoke.

"My father... the Emir... he is asleep... and I cannot wake him!"

Chapter Thirteen

How Will had a Conversation and avoided a Conflagration, and how Humfrey began his Inquestigation.

Night hung over the Dark Forest. Shayde was sitting on a horse at the head of a wide valley. Will, saddle-sore and weary, sat alongside her on his donkey.

"Wretch!" Shayde cried. "Serf! Are you here again? Pan-scourer! Spit-turner! Ladle-washer! Get back to your kitchen, saucy knave!"

Will gritted his teeth and bowed to her as civilly as his position on the donkey's back would allow. "Lady, all the way from Dun Indewood you have insulted me and ordered me to abandon this quest. You can say what you like, but I will not leave you. I have undertaken to rescue your mistress, and I will do so or die in the attempt."

"*You* will rescue her, Sir Dishwasher?" Shayde laughed scornfully. "I think not. As soon as you clap eyes on the beast that holds my mistress captive, your coward's heart will fail you; not for all the greasy broth you have ever supped nor all the gristly scraps you have ever begged would you meet a dragon face to face!"

Will bit back a furious retort. Instead, he said mildly, "I have met dragons before."

"Have you? I bet they laughed." Shayde gave Will a contemptuous glance. "Look at yourself!"

Will did so – and gasped! His battered and rusty armour had been transformed into a costume made up entirely of kitchen implements. His shins were protected by toast racks and his thighs by cheese graters and vegetable slicers. His breastplate was now two saucepan lids, with a tray to protect his stomach. The pauldrons were jelly moulds, and when Will lifted the helm from his head, he discovered that it was a stewpot, with strings dangling from its handles to fasten under his chin.

Shayde laughed heartily at Will's disgusted expression. "What better armour for a kitchen Knyght?" she cried. "Flee, my Lord Lie-by-the-Hearth, while there is yet time!"

Will seethed inwardly. If this was another of the Knyghtmare's ways of trying to humiliate him, it wasn't going to work. Furiously, he concentrated – and the cumbersome armour vanished, to be replaced by Will's own chain hauberk and battered breastplate. It was rusty, and in places paper thin, but it had served him well in many battles. And he still had his sword. After a moment's thought, he concentrated again – and felt his neck strain to take the weight of a new, stout helmet. A dragon was a formidable opponent, after all.

Shayde inclined her head in mock salute. "Very well, Sir Scullion. If you are determined to seek death, there stands the tower where my mistress lies." She pointed. Straining his eyes to penetrate the darkness, Will could just make out a tall, slender tower set halfway along the valley, part way up one of its grassy sides. "You will find the dragon asleep at its foot." Shayde leant closer to Will and hissed, "Take the beast's head off before it wakes, you were best; indeed, I deem it your only chance."

Will dismounted from his donkey and bowed. "Thank you for your advice," he said icily, "but whatever you may say, I am a Knyght of Dun Indewood – a truer Knyght than those who would not heed your call. And I have known dragons. I would never do anything so dishonourable as attack one while it slept."

Shayde drew herself up haughtily. "Then you are a great fool, as well as a knave. Farewell, Knyght of the Greasy Spoon!" She wheeled her horse and trotted away.

In an instant, Will found himself near the base of the tower. The cold, grey light of a false dawn illuminated the scene before him.

The dragon lay curled around the tower's foot, its head blocking the only door. Will began to regret his proud words to Shayde: the dragon was a fearsome-looking beast – young, lithe and supple. Will's armour could not hope to withstand its razor claws or fiery breath. His only real chance was to lop its head off while it slept. The temptation was great but Will, whose hand had wandered towards the hilt of his sword apparently of its own accord, drew it back. He settled on the grass, facing the dragon, and waited.

As the sun rose, the dragon opened one great golden eye and yawned. Will started, causing his visor to snap shut. He wondered whether the fearsome beast had really been asleep, or only pretending.

"What dost thou here, manling?" the dragon asked in a lazy voice.

Gathering his wits, Will scrambled to his feet and bowed courteously. "I have come to rescue the Lady in yonder tower. Will you give her up?"

The dragon yawned again with elaborate unconcern, and scratched itself. *"I will not."*

"Then I must challenge you to single combat."

The dragon gazed at Will with one bright, sardonic eye. *"Hmmm. Ready meal in a can... just heat and serve."* It stretched like a gigantic, scaly cat. *"Your proposal is acceptable."* Without warning, it leapt.

But Will's reflexes had been honed by many desperate battles with the denizens of the Dark Forest. He had been waiting for just such a move, and his sideways leap and roll took him out of harm's way. As he rolled, he swung his sword, but the blade merely glanced off the dragon's scales.

Hissing angrily at its prey's escape, the dragon turned

with lightning speed and belched a gout of fiery breath at Will. But once again, its intended victim was no longer there. Will had dodged to one side as soon as he had seen the jaws gape and the tiny blue flame of the pilot light, and the dragon succeeded only in baking a wide area of grass to ash.

The dragon let out a roar of frustration. *"Stand still and fight like a man!"*

"And be roasted like a chicken?" said Will. "Sorry, dragon, it's not going to happen." He ducked between the creature's legs and swung his sword again; this time his efforts were rewarded by his success in dislodging a scale from the dragon's flank. The beast roared with pain and lunged at Will, but its teeth snapped on empty air as, once again, Will's superior agility carried him beyond its reach.

But Will knew that this was a fight he could not win. He was faster than the dragon, but the fiery creature was bigger, more formidably armed and possessed of far greater strength and stamina than any human. Will would tire long before it did, and when that happened...

In the event, it happened almost immediately. The dragon unfurled its great, leathery wings, preparing to launch an aerial attack. This gave Will an opportunity: if he could evade the creature's first swoop, he might be able to reach the now-unguarded door to the tower. But as the dragon took off, and he spun to evade it, his foot caught in a tussock of grass and he fell. He was up again in a second, but although his momentary stumble caused the dragon to overshoot, its barbed tail swung round in a sweeping arc. Slamming into the side of Will's helmet, the blow sent it spinning from his head and knocked him sprawling to the ground.

Half-stunned, Will attempted to rise as the dragon drew a deep breath preparing to blast him into a fiery cinder – but at its first sight of Will's face, it suddenly checked, rearing up in astonishment. Abruptly realising that it couldn't hold its breath any longer, the great beast coughed – and a bush halfway up the hillside erupted in a ball of flame.

"I know thee!" The dragon's voice was indistinct: the interruption to its fiery breath had made it choke much as humans might if they swallowed food the wrong way. It spat out a piece of clinker and said more clearly, *"Thou art the human who returned the Dragonsbane to my kind."*

Will blinked. He had indeed returned the magical stone to Greywing, the Dragon of the Ragged Mountain, but he hadn't known that this was common knowledge among the other dragons of the Dark Forest – let alone dream dragons.

"My name is Brightscale," continued the dragon. *"My brood-sister is Darkscale, hoard-mate to Greywing."* It inclined its great head in a faintly reproving manner. *"We have met – in a manner of speaking."*

Will remembered the night that he and the Runemaster had, by the power of the Dragonsbane, shared Brightscale's mind and watched the dragons of the Dark Forest through his eyes. He struggled somewhat shakily to his feet and bowed. "I ask your pardon for my discourtesy."

"Thou hast made amends many times over," said the dragon,

but it looked troubled. *"I have no wish to fight thee,"* it said, *"but I do not see how it can be avoided. I have sworn to guard this tower against all Knyghts-errant."*

"And I have sworn to enter it, come what may."

"Then, regrettably, we must fight and one must die."

Will thought hard. Although he tried to be a Good Knyght according to the Knyghtly code, he had never finished Knyght School, had never been dubbed, never kept vigil over his armour, never had a coat of arms made by the heralds. If he was a Knyght at all, it was only because in his heart, he believed he was.

Will laid down his sword. He unbuckled the straps on his breastplate and put it aside. He shrugged off his chain hauberk and laid it on the ground. Wearing only his tunic and britches, he said, "You have vowed to keep the tower against Knyghts-errant. But I am a mere kitchen lad. Keeping me from the tower was no part of your oath. I pray you, of your courtesy, let me pass."

He braced himself to face the dragon's scorn, but it never came. In fact, he realised that the dragon's gaze, as it rested full on him, was if anything more respectful than before.

The beast bowed its huge head. *"I salute thee, Will the kitchen lad. Enter and welcome."*

Stepping round the dragon's huge muzzle, Will approached the tower.

"I have told you where I was, boggart. I was in my apartments. Meditating." Though Vizier Shaman was practically quivering with indignation, his voice was level. "I had many slights and indignities to meditate upon," he added in a savage mutter.

"But you were alone?" Humfrey persisted. The Vizier, glaring at him, nodded. Humfrey said nothing, but rubbed the sides of his mouth (a habit of his when he was thinking deeply). His attention remained on the luxurious bed where the ruler of Beau Revere, Emir Raj, lay snoring gently in a sleep that, despite the best efforts of the city's physicians and Dream Readers, had proved unbreakable. Shayde remained kneeling by her father's side, watching over him with unexpected tenderness.

A group of servants entered bearing Will's sleeping body on a stretcher, and set it down on the marble floor not far from the Emir's bed. Scrape followed them in.

Humfrey raised a hand to forestall the Vizier's protest. "My ordersh. It'sh eashier to watch the two of them if they're in the shame room." Shayde eyed the sleeping Will with a jealous disapproval that boded no good for their future attachment.

Shaman was not placated. "Your arrangement makes sense." The Vizier pointed at Scrape. "But I see no necessity for *him* to be here."

"The stranger girl told me to look after the stranger youth," said Scrape in a defiant voice that trembled very slightly, "so I did." He gazed mournfully at Will. "I tried telling him jokes, and hitting him on the head with my bladder, but nothing seemed to help."

Humfrey took the jester's stringy arm and steered him

to the door. "I'm sure you did your besht, thank you, we'll take it from here." He closed the door firmly on Scrape's disgruntled face. "OK," he said briskly, turning to face the Vizier. "I want you to do a dream reading on the kid." He tapped Will disrespectfully on the temple with a gnarled knuckle. "Let'sh shee what'sh going on in there." He gave the Emir a considering glance. "I'd like to know what'sh going on in hish mind too, but that meansh we'll need another Dream Reader in here..."

"That will not be necessary." Shayde stood up and tilted her chin proudly. "I am a Dream Reader."

Humfrey's eyebrows rose. "You don't shay?"

"Of course," said Shayde haughtily. "All families whose members are eligible to be Emir are Readers, trained at the University of Dreams."

"Ish that sho?" Humfrey's eyes narrowed with calculation. "*You* know how to contact dreamersh, huh? Intereshting..." The boggart considered for a moment before deciding. "OK. Let'sh do it."

Shayde sent one of the servants for a dream viewer and the other servants left. As the Vizier was busying himself setting up the crystal globe he had brought from the audience chamber, Rose slipped into the room carrying the Harp. With a jerk of the head, she summoned Humfrey to a whispered consultation.

Humfrey scowled at the Harp. "Did you have to bring that overshized banjo in here?"

"Hey there, big feller," said the Harp sarcastically. "It's really average to see you, too."

"I couldn't leave it in Will's room," said Rose defensively. "The Vizier wants to burn it."

"Hah!" Humfrey grinned maliciously. "I knew shooner or later he and I would agree on shomething."

The Harp stared woodenly at Humfrey. "You should meet this jester I know. You could have a not-funny competition."

Ignoring this, Humfrey jerked his thumb over his shoulder at the Vizier and Shayde. "Did you check out their shtories?"

"Yes. As far as I could. Shaman may have gone straight to his apartments and stayed there, as he says he did. I can't find anyone who saw him anywhere else in the palace until he came bursting into Will's room breathing fire." Rose shrugged. "That doesn't prove he didn't leave his rooms, of course. There are all sorts of rumours about secret passages and hidey-holes in the palace." She threw a nervous glance over her shoulder.

"What about the girl?"

"She took me to the women's quarters," the Harp put in, "just like she said she did." It gave an oily chuckle. "Those concubines, let me tell ya—"

Rose put a hand over its mouth. The Harp struggled, twanging discordantly. "She did go there," she told Humfrey, "but that was a long time before I saw her outside her apartments, and I can't find anyone who saw her between times." She glanced towards Shayde who, having received her dream viewer, was setting the globe on a cushion near the sleeping Emir.

Humfrey sighed. "Which putsh ush right back to shquare one." He turned to face the room at large and raised his voice. "Attention, pleashe!" Shayde favoured him with an insolent stare. The Vizier looked affronted. Ignoring their reactions, Humfrey said, "Now that we have the chief victimsh together in one room, in addition to the chief shushpectsh..." Humfrey grinned at the outburst of indignation from Shaman and Shayde, and waited for it to subside before going on. "Up 'til now, I've been ashking myshelf, 'who dosed Will'sh bedtime drink with bye-bye juice?', becaushe up 'til now, he'sh been the only victim. But suddenly there are two victimsh, and it'sh been clear all along that the bad guy'sh aim washn't primarily to get at Will – after all, thish malarkey shtarted way before Will and Roshe ever came here."

The Vizier waved a hand dismissively. "So much is obvious."

"Yeah – sho why did Will get attacked? Who shtands to benefit if the kid shtays ashleep? The pershon who controlsh the Knyghtmare, that'sh who. The chances are that the wise guy who put the knockout dropsh in Will'sh drink ish alsho reshponshible for bringing the Knyghtmare to Beau Revere."

"I agree," said the Vizier. "But none of this tells us who that person is."

"No. But doping Will'sh drink had two effectsh: it got Will out of the way and tied Roshe up looking after him, jusht ash they were beginning to ashk awkward questionsh; and it diverted our attention away from the real purposhe of the pershon behind the Knyghtmare – to overthrow the Emir and seize power in Beau Revere."

The Vizier gaped at Humfrey for a moment. Then, slowly, he nodded. "Your reasoning is sound, O boggart. We have been so busy dealing with the effects of the Knyghtmare's incursions, we have given too little attention to the cause."

Shayde's eyes were flashing dangerously. "But who would wish to drive my father from his throne?"

"Maybe," said Humfrey, "shomebody who thinksh he shouldn't be on it in the firsht place. But thish ish sheer shpeculation. Let'sh find shome evidence, whaddaya shay? And we'll shtart by finding out what the Knyghtmare ish up to right now."

The Vizier nodded. Sitting on the edge of the bed, he placed Will's limp right hand on the globe, holding it in position with his left. After a final, sulky glare at Humfrey and Rose, Shayde did the same with her father's hand.

Humfrey, Rose and the Harp watched, spellbound as clouds roiled within the clear globes of the dream viewers. Slowly, the clouds broke and pictures began to form...

Chapter Fourteen

How Will discovered that Hair-pulling is
No Way to Treat a Lady (even a Loathly
one).

There was no door.

Will stared at the featureless wall in amazement. There
had been a door at the foot of the tower while he was
fighting the dragon, he was sure of that – but now, there
was no trace of one. Will tried to imagine the door in its
former position, but it obstinately refused to reappear.
Perhaps the Knyghtmare's power over him was increasing.

He turned to consult Brightscale – and the dragon had
gone too. So had Will's armour. There was no trace of
Will's rusty breastplate, or his mail shirt, or his sword. For
a moment he was baffled, but then he shrugged. This was

the dream world after all. There was no point in worrying about strange things happening – weird was normal, here.

Will stared up at the single window at the top of the tower – was there movement? Yes! Someone – or something – was watching him! Will cupped his hands to his mouth. "Helllllooooooo!"

After a slight pause, a woman's head appeared at the window. She was wearing a tall, pointy hat with a veil, of the sort that Will had seen in pictures from books of Knyghtly deeds. He assumed it was the Lady that Shayde had brought him here to rescue. He could see nothing of her features, but she seemed to have an astonishing amount of shining golden hair.

Her voice, high and remote, wafted down to him. "Yes?"

Will felt rather foolish – he hadn't really thought this far ahead. "Er... are you all right up there?"

"Fine. Thank you for asking."

Will was nonplussed. "But didn't you send your damsel to the court for help?"

"Well, yes, but I told her to bring a daring Knyght-errant to rescue me, and you don't look like one of those."

"Why not?" demanded Will, rather put out.

"Well, it's mostly the fact that you seem to be standing there pretty much in your underwear, and you have no charger, and no armour, and no sword. Now, I'm no expert, but it seems to me that to be a Knyght-errant you'd need to have those things – or at least two out of three."

Will couldn't argue with this. His battered armour and his notched sword had disappeared, and the donkey hadn't been a charger no matter how far you stretched the definition. Feeling rather sheepish, he said, "Look, I really am here to rescue you. How do I get up there?"

"I'm afraid you don't."

"Well... er... what happens if you want to come down?"

"I'm not allowed. I am imprisoned here by the will of an evil enchantress."

Will gritted his teeth. All the books of chivalry he had ever read agreed that a Knyght should never think ill of a Lady; but, Will thought, if the authors of those books had ever come across a Lady as dim as this one, they might have taken a different view. "Does this enchantress come and visit you?"

"Yes. Sometimes."

"Then how does she get up there?" demanded Will, who was rapidly running out of patience. "On a broomstick?"

"Are you being sarcastic? I don't like sarcastic people."

Will controlled his temper with an effort. "Please tell me how she gets up there."

"Oh, she just calls me to let down my hair, and then she climbs up it."

Will blinked. "You let down your hair?" He thought for a moment. "It must be very long."

"Oh, it is. I have to brush it ever such a lot."

"Yes, I suppose you would."

"Otherwise it gets tangled, you see."

"Ah."

"Forty-seven times each side."

"As much as that?" said Will, who was wondering

whether rescuing this Lady might be more trouble than it was worth. But then he reminded himself that Knyghts didn't think like that. Anyway, this was part of his quest – and a promise was a promise after all. "Can I come up there?" he called.

The Lady gave an apologetic shrug. "I'm afraid not."

"You could let down your hair."

"I can't do that unless you say the magic rhyme."

"Magic rhyme?"

"Yes, it makes my hair grow."

"I thought your hair..."

The Lady gave an extraordinarily irritating laugh. "Oh, it's not long enough to reach the ground all the time, you silly boy. If it was, it would be so piled up in here there wouldn't be room for me!"

Will was beginning to wonder whether all the power of the Lady's brain went into growing her hair. She certainly didn't seem to use it for thinking. "Well, what is the magic rhyme?"

"You say my name twice, and then you say,

Let down your hair
That I may climb the golden stair."

"All right," said Will patiently. "What is your name?"

"Oh, I'm afraid I can't tell you that."

Will clenched his fists in exasperation.

"I'm not allowed," said the Lady. "That's part of the enchantment. You can guess if you like, but you probably won't guess right because I have a very unusual name, and lots of Knyghts have been here before you, and they've all guessed names like Matilda and Belinda and Eleanor, but none of them has guessed that my real name is Rapunzel." Her hand flew to her mouth. "Oops!"

Will grinned to himself. "So all I have to do is call out:

Rapunzel, Rapunzel,
Let down your hair
That I may climb the golden stair—"

He broke off as the Lady tilted her head to one side and a waterfall of golden hair cascaded down the side of the tower until it brushed the grass at his feet.

The Lady sighed. "Oh well, it can't be helped. You'd better come up."

Will reached for the Lady's hair. He took a handful in each fist and pulled.

The Harp, staring into the dream viewer, cackled. "Sap! I could have told him that would happen. Simple matter of power-to-weight ratios. Clean living lad, lots of healthy fresh air and exercise – he must be at least twice as heavy as some old witch—"

"Shut up!" snapped Rose.

"She popped out of that window like a cork!"

"Yes, I did see that, thank you."

"And then he tried to catch her! Haw haw haw!"

Rose glared at the unseemly tangle of limbs at the base of the tower and gritted her teeth. "Of all the idiotic—" She broke off. "I suppose he's all right?" she said, trying to sound casual.

"Sure he'sh all right," said Humfrey. "It'sh only a dream, remember?"

"Yes, but..." Rose cast a sidelong glance at the Vizier, who was concentrating on the dream reading and taking no apparent interest in their conversation. "...*he* said people can die in this sort of dream."

"I don't think the kid'sh dead," said Humfrey judiciously. "He wouldn't be wriggling about like that or making sho much noishe."

"Sssssh!" admonished the Harp. "I want to hear how the big lunk tries to talk his way out of this one..."

Will groaned. "Get off! You're squashing me."

The Lady bridled. "Are you implying that I'm overweight?"

"I'm sure your weight is absolutely perfect – I just wish you'd take it somewhere else!"

The Lady sniffed and stood up. "Well, that's not the sort of remark I'd expect from a Knyght-errant, I must say."

Will dragged himself into a sitting position and felt

gingerly for broken bones. Finding none, he gave a sigh of relief – and then looked up at the Lady. As the mass of hair she had let fall shrivelled like burning thatch, exposing her face, his jaw dropped.

The Lady was the most hideous crone he had ever seen. She stared back at him. "What?"

"You're... er... older than I thought you'd be."

The Lady darted forward. Will recoiled from her pointy chin and crooked, warty nose. "What are you saying? That I'd only have deserved to be rescued if I was young and beautiful?"

Will eyed the Lady's horrendous features, taking in the wrinkled skin, greasy hair and yellow, bloodshot eyes, and tried without much success to hide his disgust. Of course he wasn't thinking that – not exactly – but he couldn't help feeling that there were limits. In a bid to placate the Lady, Will said, "At least, you're down from that tower. It's not the sort of rescue I had in mind," he admitted, "but it seems to have worked."

"Oh, you haven't rescued me yet," said the Lady. She gave a nasty cackle. "That was the easy part. But to break the enchantress's spell, there's one more thing you have to do."

With an unflattering lack of enthusiasm, Will said, "Oh? What's that?"

"You have to marry me."

Instantly Will found himself in a chapel.

He was standing beside the Lady, who was wearing a bridal gown over her skinny body, with flowers (already wilting) in her greasy hair. A priest stood at the altar below an intricately-leaded window, through which the light of the setting sun fell upon Will and his grotesque bride. Will looked over his shoulder – and caught a glimpse of an expectant-looking congregation – before the Lady tugged firmly at his arm, bringing him back to the matter in hand.

Will gawped at her. "Just a minute! I promised to rescue you – nobody said anything about getting married."

"Tough," said the Lady. "It's all part of the deal."

"But I don't even *know* you!"

The Lady grinned maliciously at him. "Is that the only reason you don't want to marry me?"

Well, thought Will, the fact that you're hideous beyond description is a bit off-putting, to be brutally honest – but that wasn't the sort of thing a Good Knyght could say to a Lady. So he just muttered, "It's all a bit sudden."

"Oh, well, if that's all..."

Outside, the sun set. As the last rays faded, a change came over the Lady. Her wrinkles faded, her limbs straightened, her hair grew dark and luxurious – and Will gave a gasp of astonishment as Shayde – beautiful and deceitful – stood beside him.

"Yes, Lord of the Stewpots," she said in soft, mocking tones, "I am both the damsel who brought you here, and the Lady you swore to rescue. Will you indeed marry me and break the curse?" she demanded, taunting him. "And if so, what would you have me be? Foul by day, fair by night? Or foul or fair the whole time? Choose, Sir Knyght."

Time stood still. Will thought furiously.

How had Shayde got into the tower and become Rapunzel? He shook his head, reminding himself yet again that this was the dream world: normal rules didn't apply. In any case, what mattered now was the decision he had to make, for Will now understood that this was the Knyghtmare's challenge.

In her daytime guise as an old woman, the Lady was frightful to look at and not very clever – but she'd seemed straightforward. In her Shayde form, she was beautiful and intelligent – but malicious, scornful and not to be trusted. And the Lady was right: Will had promised to rescue her. What she looked like was neither here nor there. As for choosing what form she should take...

Will looked the Lady straight in the eye. "I shall marry you, for that is what I promised. As for what I would have you be..." Will shook his head. "That is not for me to say. Nobody can decide for another what he or she should be. You must choose for yourself."

There was a crack of thunder. Chapel, priest, congregation, bride-to-be – all disappeared in a chorus of screams and insane laughter, and once again, Will found himself facing the black Knyght.

The Knyghtmare's horse pawed at the ground. The black Knyght's face was hidden by its visor, but its voice betrayed anger and frustration. "Once more, boy, you have guessed the riddle aright." The horse reared. Jerking savagely at its reins and jabbing unmercifully at its flanks with his spurs, the Knyghtmare brought it under control. "As you have not sought to impose your will on others, I have no power to impose mine on you... yet! But you shall not survive the next test, pig boy. You have only bought yourself time – and now that time is about to run out!"

Shayde's cry brought Rose and Humfrey across from their study of Will's dream. Shaman, though he glanced across to see what was amiss, kept most of his attention focused on Will, continuing to read his dreams.

Her eyes filled with tears, Shayde indicated the pain-wracked figure of the Emir in the dream viewer and looked up at Rose in helpless appeal. "My poor father – the Knyghtmare is torturing him."

The image in the dream viewer clearly showed that Emir Raj was in terrible pain. He was lying on a hard, comfortless bed in a bare stone room. Four windows, one on each wall, revealed that he was on an island, in the tower of a castle which was surrounded by a wilderness of dead forest, barren fields, burnt and blackened moorland. Each window showed a distant view of the sea, lying smooth and waveless under a clouded sky.

"What's wrong with him?" asked Rose.

"Take a look there." Humfrey pointed to a wound in the Emir's side which bled – not dangerously, but constantly – without showing any signs of healing. "If I'm not mishtaken, that wound was caushed by a blade – a sword or shpear thrusht."

The Emir groaned. Shayde gave a sob. "Why is the Knyghtmare tormenting him so? It is wicked... senseless..."

"Wicked, it is," said Rose slowly, "but not senseless. I think I know what the Knyghtmare is doing."

"Yeah?" said Humfrey. "Are you gonna share thish inshight with ush, or what?"

"If I'm right, it's recreating an old legend – the oldest legend in the Dark Forest. The Tale of the Maimed King."

"Hey, I know that one!" The Harp strummed importantly. "It's in the old ballads." It sang:

"Old King Hoel, he pinched a bowl,
For a greedy old soul was he;
Then a dirty great spear came up from the rear
And stabbed him in the fiddle-de-dee...!"

Rose grabbed a large, floppy cushion from the Emir's bed and wrapped it round the Harp. Speaking over the instrument's muffled protests, she said, "According to the legend, at one time many of the wells and streams in the Dark Forest were magical and had nymphs as their guardians."

"You bet they did!" cried the Harp as the cushion slipped. "Those nymphs! Hubba-hubba-hubba! Even better than concubines. I could tell you stories—"

"But you won't," snapped Rose. "Not unless you want to be whittled down to clothes pegs." She gathered her thoughts. "Anyway, one of these nymphs had a golden cup in which she offered water to thirsty travellers."

"That's right," interrupted the Harp. "But King Hoel was a thieving old buzzard. He turned up at the well gasping with thirst and the nymph gave him a drink from her cup, but instead of giving it back he took off like a deer with an arrow in the backside."

"Will you let me tell this story?" demanded Rose.

"Oh, so suddenly *you're* the storyteller round here?" sneered the Harp. "That's gotta make sense. Obviously you know more about legends etcetera than I do, even though singing ballads and lays is my sole purpose in life – but please, don't let the fact that you're robbing my existence of any meaning stand in your way!"

"All right," said Rose off-handedly, and went on. "As the King rode from the well, a flying spear appeared from nowhere and struck him in the side—"

"Hey, I was being ironic! You didn't have to take me literally!"

"When this happened, the cup disappeared and so did all the nymphs. Their wells and streams dried up, and the King's country became a wasteland. Animals died, crops failed, the people despaired."

Shayde had been listening intently to the story. "Where did this happen?" she asked.

Rose shrugged. "Maybe the Harp knows."

"Oh, great!" whined the Harp. "You steal one of my best stories, you blow the punchline, now you want details..."

"So you *don't* know."

"Well, no," admitted the Harp sulkily. "But the legend says that the old King is still lying in the Castle of the Fountain, and he can only be cured if the best Knyght in the Forest offers him a drink from the stolen cup."

"And I guessh you don't know where thish Cashtle of the Fountain ish, either?"

"Nobody does exactly," said Rose, ignoring the Harp's aggrieved mutterings. "In the old days, lots of Knyghts died trying to find it. All the legend says is that it has four corners, and it stands on an island surrounded by water and is very difficult to reach."

"Sho if you're right," said Humfrey, "the Knyghtmare hash shet the Emir up ash thish Maimed King, and the only way he can get cured ish if Will manages to get to the cashtle (even though nobody knowsh where it ish), prove he'sh the besht Knyght in the Foresht, find thish cup watchamacallit that nobody'sh ever sheen, and get the old geezer to drink from it before he pegsh out."

"That's about the size of it," said Rose grimly.

Shayde, watching her father in the dream viewer, stifled another sob. Humfrey stared at the Emir and gave a low whistle. "Boy, ish *he* in trouble!" Then his gaze hardened. "Brace yourshelves, boysh and girlsh. Looksh like the old guy hash company."

The black Knyght had appeared, out of nowhere, in the Emir's dream. As it stood beside the east window of the chamber, its visor turned towards the observers for a moment as if its hidden eyes were gazing directly into theirs. Then the Knyghtmare directed its attention to the pain-wracked figure on the bed. "You are powerless," it taunted. "You are weak. You rule nothing."

The Emir opened his eyes. Gasping with the effort, he

lifted himself on to one elbow and managed to say, "Who are you?"

The black Knyght gave a mirthless laugh. "Your enemy... unto death." Its laughter grew until it filled the chamber, echoing from wall to wall in a cacophony of scorn and spite.

But the Emir seemed barely to hear it. Following his gaze, Rose stifled a gasp, and Humfrey's mouth curved into a ferocious grin. Framed in the window at the Knyghtmare's side – still far away but drawing steadily nearer – was a ship, moving without sail or oars across the unruffled water of the sea. A lone figure stood in the prow, gazing towards the barren island and its castle. From the tower, the pained Emir watched its approach, his expression alive with dawning hope.

CHAPTER FIFTEEN

H ow the Castle went Round and the Traitor
was Found.

T he ship grounded on shingle. Will gathered himself and leapt into the shallows.

The island was wreathed in mist. Dense grey vapours oozed from the ground to hang sullenly over the barren earth. Above them, the bare branches of trees, as lifeless as though struck by lightning, formed agonised, contorted shapes against the leaden sky. Behind them, in the distance, reared the grim stone walls of the castle. The soft hiss of water on the black stones of the beach, and the raucous cries of gore crows circling overhead, were the only sounds to be heard in all that barren land.

A tangle of dead briars and brambles blocked his way. Will crouched and began to crawl through the obstruction...

...and suddenly found himself far from the shore. A great tree spread its branches over him – massive, noble, lifeless. At its foot, a spring bubbled out of the rock, its water collecting in a crude stone basin which overflowed to form a tiny stream, wending away into the devastation. Beside the basin, on a slab of marble, stood a golden vessel that might have been a small bowl or a large cup. The outside was decorated with six identical heads – perhaps of kings, or of gods of the Old Forest. The inside was inscribed with different scenes: mythical beasts – gryphons and wyverns; warriors – hunting, marching and riding to war; men in robes blowing strange dragon-headed, trumpet-like instruments that reared above them like snakes about to strike.

"Pretty, isn't it?" said a voice behind him.

Will spun round. "Rose!" He had to fight an almost irresistible impulse to hug her. Then his face fell. "What are you doing here?"

Rose gave him a bright smile. "I thought you might need some help, so I went to sleep."

Will groaned. "You shouldn't have done that! What if the Vizier sends somebody to knock us on the head...?"

Rose laughed. "Relax! Humfrey's here – at least, he's in Beau Revere. He's looking after things, and I think he's pretty close to finding out who's behind the Knyghtmare."

Will's jaw dropped. "But how did Humfrey...?"

"I don't know. He must have heard about what was happening to us somehow. Does it matter? The point is, I came to tell you what's going on in your dream so you'd know what to do."

Will listened intently as Rose told him the story of the Maimed King, though he hardly needed to be reminded of it. It was one of the most famous legends of the Dark Forest – the tale of the Golden Cup had been in all the books of Knyghtly lore.

"When King Hoel died," Rose concluded, "the chief men of his court returned the cup to the fountain, but the nymph never came back and the curse was never lifted."

Will reached out and picked up the golden vessel, handling it with reverence. "And it's still here!" He looked up at Rose. "But what am I supposed to do with it?"

"Well, the legend says you have to fill the cup with water and pour it out on the slab."

"What happens then?"

"I don't know. Why don't you do it and we'll find out."

Holding his breath, Will dipped the cup into the basin and tilted it so that the water fell splashing on to the marble.

Instantly, there was a peal of thunder so terrific that it made his ears ring. Rose cried out and clapped her hands to her head...

...and they found themselves at the castle. The cup had vanished. Before them stood the black Knyght.

The Knyghtmare saluted Will mockingly. "Well met Lord – and Lady." The armoured figure gestured to the tower behind him. "And welcome to the Castle of the Fountain. You may enter... if you can."

From the corner of his mouth, Will said to Rose, "You're sure the Emir is in there?" Rose nodded. Raising his voice, Will said, "I shall. Let us pass."

"By all means." The black Knyght stood aside. Behind him was a door – a plain, wooden door. Will stepped forward.

There was a grinding noise. Before Will's astonished eyes, the wall of the castle began to move. The great, ponderous mass of stone was turning on its own axis, as if it were revolving on a potter's wheel. The door was now some distance away, and retreating further by the minute. Will turned to Rose, who looked as bewildered as he was. Should he run after the door – try to chase it, open it on the move and hurl himself through it like someone trying to board a moving coach? But a moment's reflection showed him the castle was moving too fast for that.

The Knyghtmare's mocking laughter pounded at his ears. "My Castle of the Fountain has many names – among them, the Castle of Riches, the Castle of Glass... and the Revolving Castle. Step closer, Sir Knyght – and be dashed to pieces!"

"Will!" Rose was clutching at his arm. "Come away! You'll be killed!"

By now, the castle was turning so fast that its walls were no more than a blur. Will stood, lost in thought.

"Will!" Rose tugged harder.

Without taking his eyes from the castle, Will grabbed

Rose's hand. "Listen! What we're seeing can't be real! A castle doesn't turn like a spinning top. It's just an illusion!" Will pointed. "The door's still there. It hasn't moved. The castle only looks as if it's spinning. If we close our eyes, we'll find the door."

"Are you mad?" There was terror in Rose's voice. "We'll be squashed like ants under a cartwheel. Will, don't..."

Ignoring her pleas, Will closed his eyes and drew Rose inexorably forward. She screamed and fought to loosen his grip. Still he went on, his right hand outstretched – until his questing fingers felt the unmistakable grain of well-seasoned wood. Feeling his way, Will closed his hand around the door handle, turned it – and he and Rose fell through the doorway. There was a bellow of rage from behind them, the door slammed shut... and then there was silence.

Rose was beside herself with rage and fright. "Don't you *ever* do that again!"

"You want me to promise never to drag you through the doorway of a spinning castle with my eyes shut? All right, I promise."

"It's not funny! What if you'd been wrong?"

Will shrugged. "I wasn't." He looked around.

"You weren't to know that! You could have got us both killed—"

"I hate to interrupt you in mid-nag," said Will, "but have you taken a look at where we are yet?"

"Don't evade the issue! I... Oh!" Rose looked around, her eyes wide. She shivered, moved closer to Will and took his hand. "Will..."

"I know."

They were in a corridor whose walls, floor and ceiling were made entirely from bone. The bones were human. Skulls with staring eye sockets and grinning jaws, ribs, shoulder and pelvic bones, thigh, shin and arm bones were cemented together, with vertebrae, finger and toe bones filling the gaps between. The bones seemed to shine from within with a strange, unwholesome luminescence, filling the corridor with dead, shadowless light.

"Oeth-Aroeth," said Will, recognising their grisly surroundings as another location from the old legends. "Another name for the Castle of the Fountain – the Castle of Bone."

"Will..." Rose's voice was a hoarse whisper. "We've got to turn back."

"We can't," said Will matter-of-factly. "The door's gone." He thought for a moment. "According to the legend, the Castle of Bone is a labyrinth. We have to find our way through it."

Rose said, "I'm scared." Will had never seen her so woebegone.

He gave her an encouraging grin. "I think that's the general idea," he said, gesturing at their gruesome surroundings. "Come on. The sooner we start, the sooner we'll be finished."

Will led the way down the echoing white corridors. So intent was he on fighting down his own rising panic, and remembering which way they had turned, that he completely failed to notice the goat hooves that peeped out, now and again, from under 'Rose's' dress.

"The witless clod!" Rose stared at Will and her double in the dream viewer, her voice rising to a screech of exasperation. "The bird-brained numbskull! The empty-headed lummox!" She turned to harangue Humfrey as though what she was witnessing was his fault. "What's the matter with him? Can't he see that drippy female isn't me?"

"Don't be too hard on the kid," said Humfrey cajolingly. "You gotta admit, itsh a pretty good likenessh."

This was a mistake. "It is *not* a good likeness!" ranted Rose. "The soft, soupy, rabbit-hearted floozy doesn't look a *bit* like me. If that meat-headed simpleton has the *cheek* to dream about me, he might at least get the details right!"

"Yeah," agreed the Harp. "For one thing, his dream version looks as if she washes on at least an annual basis and doesn't have birds nesting in her hair."

"She ishn't a she," said Humfrey quickly, as Rose reached for the Harp with an expression that made the instrument quail.

The comment brought Rose up short. "What do you mean?"

"For one thing, the kid *ishn't* dreaming about you. You're dead right about that."

"Why shouldn't he be dreaming about me? He's been dreaming about Shayde." Rose glowered at the Emir's daughter who, oblivious to her antagonism, was gazing avidly into the viewer showing her father's dream.

"Yesh, but ash an enemy, not an ally. The Knyghtmare hash been putting Shayde into Will'sh dreamsh but using her hashn't done it any good, sho my guessh ish it'sh changing tacticsh."

Rose pointed at the 'Rose' who was following Will through the ghastly white corridors of the Castle of Bone. "But if she isn't me, who is she?"

"Check out the hooves."

Rose's eyes widened, her jaw dropped, and she said, in a horrified voice, "Oh, blood and bones! She's a fetch!"

The Vizier, intent on reading Will's dream, had not spoken for some time. Now, unexpectedly, he said, "What is a fetch?"

Rose, staring in dismay at the scene in the dream viewer, made no reply. Humfrey said, "It'sh a kind of hobgoblin. It can take on a human shape, but there'sh alwaysh one thing that gives it away – in thish case, the fake Rose hash hooves inshtead of feet."

"If you ask me," said the Harp, "it's an improvement. Hooves don't smell."

The Vizier gave a slight nod. "And what is the purpose of this deception?"

"To lead people astray," said Humfrey. "It'sh trying to get Will to trusht it – and when he doesh, it'll lure him into danger—"

He broke off as the door flung open behind them, apparently all by itself. There was a chill draught of air –

and Tym appeared. With an apologetic tinkle of bells, Scrape slipped into the room behind him and hovered by the door with a mulish, hangdog expression, evidently fearful of being ordered out. The jester stood wringing his hands, his anxious eyes fixed on the Emir.

Tym glanced around the room, taking in the recumbent figures of Will and the Emir, the glowing dream viewers, Rose, Humfrey, the Harp, the Vizier – and Shayde. "It's taken me ages to find you," the Whizzard complained, his eyes lingering on the Emir's daughter. "What in the Forest is going on here?"

Introductions and explanations took some time. When Tym had been brought up to date, Humfrey said, "Sho what'sh new with you, Whizz kid?"

"Plenty," said Tym, still looking at Shayde (who, despite her anxiety for her father, was giving him a tentative half-smile in return).

Humfrey turned to the others. "Ash shoon ash I arrived here, I heard a few thingsh that shet me thinking. Sho I shent our Whizzard out into the Foresht to check out a few detailsh and shcout around..."

The Vizier looked puzzled. "Shcout around?"

"Yeah, shcout around. Keep hish eyes and earsh open. Don't interrupt." Humfrey turned back to Tym. "Find anything?"

Tym nodded. "I did what you said. I went to Whizzard speed and looked for signs of an ambush – burnt-out carts, bits of armour scattered around, that sort of thing. Nothing for seven days' travel on any road leading to Beau Revere."

Humfrey nodded as if Tym's report had confirmed his suspicions. "But I found something else. Some way to the west of here I found a deserted village. It was in terrible shape. Lots of the buildings had been destroyed by fire. Crops were going to seed – nothing had been gathered. There were dead animals just lying about; the ones that were still alive were roaming around wild. And there were people..." Tym hesitated.

Humfrey said, grimly, "Go on."

"Well – they were like savages. They were filthy and their clothes were falling off them. They were terrified – of everything, as far as I could see: of me, of each other, of their own shadows. They were living like animals in the ruins and the edges of the Forest, eating anything they could find, raw – and their eyes!" Tym shuddered. "When I popped up out of nowhere, they all ran off, screaming that the Knyghtmare had come again!"

Humfrey nodded again. "That'sh the missing piece of the puzzle." Without looking around, the boggart said in conversational tones, "Hey, Shcrape! Sheeing ash you're here, hand me that piece of parchment and the inkwell and quill by the door, willya?"

Hesitantly, the jester complied. As he folded the parchment into three, Humfrey continued, "I've lived in the Foresht a long time, and I never heard of any other city between here and Dun Indewood. A few villages and hamletsh, maybe, but no city. Sho I kinda wondered about the shtory Shcrape told me when I firsht got here – all that shtuff about being ambushed." He tore the parchment into three equal strips, then folded each strip into four and tore along the folds. "I shent Tym off to check it out and then I remembered shomething Runie showed me back in Dun Indewood. Shomething called an anagram. Lemme demonshtrate."

Surrounded by fascinated silence, Humfrey dipped his quill into the ink. On each of the twelve pieces of parchment, he wrote a single letter. Then he squatted on his heels and laid them out on the floor so that they read...

"Shcrape told me he'd been ambushed in the Foresht while travelling with the lord of hish city. I don't think there ever wash a city, and I don't think there ever wash an ambush," said Humfrey matter-of-factly. "But I can guessh what happened to the village Tym found." He looked up at Scrape. "That was a dry run, washn't it? To find out how great your powersh were before you made the attempt on Beau Revere."

Humfrey's nimble fingers switched the parchment pieces about almost faster than the eye could follow. When he had finished, the letters made out the words...

Humfrey gave Scrape a wolfish grin. "Cute," he said. "You like riddles, right? The Knyghtmare ushesh them all the time in the dreamsh it sendsh. And you couldn't reshisht leaving a shtonking great clue and laughing up your shleeve when nobody worked it out, could you, wise guy?"

At a nod from Humfrey, Tym stepped forward and ripped off Scrape's three-pointed jester's cap. Bereft of its disguise, his face was unrecognisable: the anxious, put-upon expression had vanished; the weak, tremulous jaw was set in a hard, bitter line; the watery eyes sparked with malignance as they gazed at Humfrey with hateful intensity. The dark hair was tightly cropped, revealing the torn remains of an ear. The Vizier and Shayde cried aloud as they at last recognised their enemy – the old Emir's son, long presumed dead, who had been cast aside and had now returned to seize his inheritance. Jasper – the missing heir.

CHAPTER SIXTEEN

Of Dreadful Dreams and Wicked Schemes, and how Will was beset by Toads in a Hole.

"I congratulate you, Boggart." Jasper clapped his hands together in resounding and ironic applause.

"I knew he was a criminal," said the Harp triumphantly. "I knew it the moment I heard his jokes. A man who could put an audience through that sort of torture is capable of anything."

The Vizier was practically grinding his teeth. "I cannot conceive how we failed to check on his account of himself."

"Don't feel too bad," said Jasper, in mock commiseration. He spread his arms wide. "When you look at a man in a fool's costume, you don't see the man: you see only the fool." He chuckled. "And I really was a jester, you know, in the village your Whizzard discovered." He inclined his head towards Tym. "It's called Dun Fore, by the way – appropriately, as it turns out." Tym clenched his fists and took a step forwards, but was halted by a gesture from Humfrey. "Oh, yes," continued Jasper, "I progressed from village idiot to court jester. It's not a bad life – light work with regular meals – and when you come to think about it, a jester does much the same thing as the Dreamwalker... or the Knyghtmare. He reveals the follies of the rich and powerful and forces them to look within themselves. Is it the jester's fault if they don't always like what they see?"

"Murderer!" Shayde, who from the moment Scrape's true identity had been revealed had seemed too stunned to speak or move, flung herself upon her cousin, screaming with fury, biting Jasper and tearing at him with her nails. "Assassin! What have you done to my father? Carrion! The ravens shall tear the living flesh from your bones!"

By the time Tym and Rose (neither of them trying terribly hard) had managed to drag Shayde away and subdue her, Jasper was looking considerably the worse for wear. His nose was bleeding and his one good ear looked as though it had escaped the fate of its companion by a whisker. Jasper's eyes blazed as he wiped blood from his face. He turned his gaze to the dream viewer next to the Emir – and the figure within the globe gave an anguished moan as blood burst from his wound. Shayde gave a cry of dismay and flung her arms around her father, who groaned pitifully in his sleep.

"Presume to lay a finger on me once more, witch, and your father dies in both worlds," snarled Jasper. Shayde's eyes burned with hate, but she said nothing.

Humfrey rubbed his chin. "Shuppose you tell ush what you've been up to all theshe yearsh? How'sh about you shtart with the fire."

Jasper laughed unpleasantly. "Oh, I started that, of course. Nobody from Beau Revere goes out into the Forest if they can help it, but I knew that if I just wandered off, there would be attempts to find me. So I set fire to the palace and faked my own death. It was a rotten palace anyway."

"People died," said the Vizier in a carefully controlled voice.

Jasper shrugged. "Servants. Guards. No one of any account." Rose stared at him, her lips set in a grimace of distaste.

Humfrey said, "And then you shkedaddled. But why did you want to dishappear in the firsht place?"

"To avoid discovery," said Jasper easily. "By the Dreamwalker, or by my own dear family. You see, I was a Dream Reader – as are all my family – but I found that I could do more than read dreams. I could *influence* them – mould them. Eventually, I discovered that I could *create* them."

The Vizier's face was pale. "But nobody has the power to create dreams," he said in a voice that barely rose above a whisper. "Only the Dreamwalker…" He tailed off. In the dream viewer at his side, the tiny figures of Will and 'Rose' made their way, unregarded, through the maze of bone.

"Precisely." Jasper's smile was horrible to see. "At first I had some fun with my abilities – settling a few scores, that sort of thing. But then I began to wonder what my dear father would do if he found out the extent of my powers. Exploit them for his own benefit? Not he – an honest fool my father, like his Vizier, the enlightened and merciful Shaman. They would fear me. And what then? Would they have me beheaded? Or thrown from the highest tower in the city? Or would they merely have me blinded and left in the deepest dungeon to rot? I found none of the alternatives pleasing.

"But my father was ailing and once I was Emir who would dare touch me? Then, at the moment I believed myself safe, the cup of victory was dashed from my lips. On his deathbed, my father disinherited me and threw away the throne on the fat fool who lies groaning there." Shayde hissed at Jasper like a cat.

"Sho you lammed out before the Dream Readersh shmelled a rat."

Jasper nodded. "I wandered for days. I will admit to you that I was terrified. There were always shadows beneath the trees – rustlings in the bushes. I had heard of the horrors that lived out in the Forest. But none came near me."

"Some things," said Shayde harshly, "even dogs will not stoop to eat."

Jasper gave her an angry glare, but continued calmly, "Eventually, I found the village of Dun Fore. The people took me in."

"Tough break for them," said the Harp.

"Think you so?" snapped Jasper. "Do you imagine they were kind to me? They laughed at my clothes, and at my manner of speaking. They spurned me, and gave me menial and humiliating jobs – I, who was once the heir to Beau Revere! They set me to look after their pigs…"

"I know someone who once looked after pigs for a living," said Rose. "He survived it."

"And so did I. But I eventually realised I could turn even the scorn of my enemies into a weapon I could use. If I could not avoid their laughter, I would court it… and, ultimately, control it. And so from idiot I became fool and jester to the Lord of Dun Fore – a rustic oaf, but with the power to protect me. And I waited.

"And at the same time, I exercised my power over the dreaming mind. Dreams I sent – such dreams!" Jasper cackled. "Those who mocked me and spurned me soon had cause to wish they had never been born – but of course, they never imagined that the night terrors that caused them to fly, screaming, from their beds were sent by their poor, weak, foolish jester.

"The people of Dun Fore had a legend of a black Knyght who kept the passage of a ford against all comers. I adopted the Knyghtmare as my representative in the dream world."

"And shoon," said Humfrey, "you learnt to control many

dreamsh at once. Then you were ready. You wormed your way into Beau Revere."

"Yes, thanks to the foolishness of my father's choice of Emir. Shaman might have been more suspicious if I had not taken such care to annoy him – irritation is a powerful enemy of thought, as is contempt. And my dear cousin Shayde might have recognised me, had she not been so preoccupied with finding a way out of her engagement to Shaman. But in any case, a jester's motley covers a multitude of sins, and I had my disguise pretty much perfect by then. I am even persuaded that it is part of my power to be able to disguise not only my thoughts and plans, but my features. In any case, I returned to Beau Revere in the guise of jester Scrape."

"Having first driven mad the people of Dun Fore, who took you in when you were starving." Tym's voice shook.

"Yes," said Jasper calmly. "Why not? They had ill-treated me. They were barbarians. And I had to test my powers. Once I had proved my strength, it was time to return to my beloved city and gradually introduce the good people of Beau Revere to the Knyghtmare. My ultimate aim was to drive the people who had rejected me insane with fear and guilt; to use the Knyghtmare to remove my father's nominee from the throne and set myself up as ruler of a city of mindless slaves."

"You musht have been pretty cheeshed off," said Humfrey, "when Will and Roshe turned up."

"Yes. Their presence nearby disturbed me. I guessed they might be less susceptible to my sendings than a Beau

Reverean. When they came on, despite the evil dreams I sent to frighten them away, my suspicions were confirmed. So I made myself seem harmless and useful, until an opportunity should arise to betray them."

"Sho you shlipped Will a Mickey Finn to shend him into the dream world, where you could deshtroy him at your leisure."

"Exactly."

The Harp whistled appreciatively. "You know, I've met some real bad hombres in my time, but you leave them standing. You are a louse's louse."

"You're too kind." Jasper bowed ironically. When he straightened, he was holding a small phial which he had apparently taken from some secret pocket in his costume. "Unhappily, I'm afraid the time has come for me to leave you." He turned to Shaman. "I caution you not to visit revenge upon my sleeping body. I shall know of it, and the torments I shall visit upon the perpetrators will be beyond imagining." He raised the phial to his lips.

"Tym!" yelled Humfrey. "It'sh shleeping potion! Shtop him!"

Tym instantly went to Whizzard speed. All motion in the room seemingly ceased and Tym stepped forward, reaching out for the phial. But already, the potion was pouring from the vessel and into Jasper's mouth. Tym knocked the phial aside – too late. In slow motion, the liquid continued to tumble down Jasper's motionless gullet. There was no way even a Whizzard could stop it.

Tym reappeared, shaking his head. "Sorry," he said.

The controller of the Knyghtmare gave a single bark of triumphant laughter – before slumping to the floor, unconscious.

Rose stared at the sleeping figure. "Why did he do that? He's sent himself into the dream world, just like he sent Will and the Emir."

"Yep," said Humfrey grimly, "but he *controlsh* the dream world, and we can't reach him there."

"He has left his body behind," said the Vizier savagely. "We can visit such revenge upon his miserable carcass, that it shall be spoken of with horror for a thousand years." Shayde nodded eagerly.

Humfrey shook his head. "It'sh an attractive proposition, but we daren't do anything to hish body while he sleepsh, and he knowsh it. He hash hostagesh – Will and the Emir. All he hash to do ish wait until hish dreamsh drive ush all crazy, then he can wake up and take control."

"Then we are helpless." The Vizier's voice was desolate.

"Not quite. Only Will can save the Emir now, and there's only one way to help Will. Someone hash to follow him into the dream world." Humfrey looked Rose straight in the eye and struck a dramatic pose. "You're our lasht hope, kid. Closhe your big baby-blue eyes and... *follow that shleeper!*"

"We must be nearly at the centre by now," said Will.

"What's the point of going on?" wailed Rose. "We'll be stuck in here for ever. I read a story," she continued accusingly, "about a hero who went into a labyrinth, and *he* laid down a trail of string from the entrance so he could follow it and find the way out."

"I read that story too," said Will, "and as I recall, it was the hero's female companion who gave him the string. I always wondered why she just happened to be carrying about a mile of string around with her. In any case, the entrance closed behind us, remember? And we're not trying to find the way out, we're trying to find the way in."

"In?"

"To the centre of the maze." Will hesitated for a moment, then stepped forward cautiously. "Speaking of which, I think we're there."

Will and Rose stepped into a small chamber. It was square in shape, otherwise it looked exactly like the corridors they had been trudging down for what seemed like hours.

Rose stood in the middle of the chamber and looked around with an expression nicely balanced between terror and disapproval. "So what happens now?"

Will turned around. "Well, it seems the first thing that happens is that the corridor we came in through disappears..."

"What?!" Rose stared around at the four unbroken walls and whimpered.

"And the second thing," said Will, listening to the

sudden rustling and scuttling sounds that seemed to come from the walls and were now echoing round the chamber, "is that something comes and attacks us."

"Like what?"

"Like that!"

"Will!"

The skulls surrounding them were suddenly alive. Snakes, in a myriad venomous colours, poured from every empty eye socket, hissing like kettles. From between grinning jaws oozed large, ugly toads. These were quite outstandingly warty and possessed of wicked-looking beaks, which they snapped viciously as they advanced in a series of splay-footed hops.

Will closed his eyes. Rose stared at him. "What are you doing?"

"I'm trying to imagine a way out of here."

"Oh, very constructive! Stop daydreaming and keep them off me!" Rose was leaping around in an attempt to avoid the creatures' darting attacks.

Will opened his eyes. No miraculous mode of escape seemed to have presented itself. The Knyghtmare's power was still growing, Will's was weakening; it came to the same thing. He was already bleeding from several toad pecks.

"Keep them off me!" repeated Rose. "Use your sword!"

"I don't have a sword! Where's your dagger?"

"I lost it!" Rose clung to Will. "I'm sorry! Save me!"

"I'd love to," said Will tightly, "but I've nothing to fight them with."

Rose screamed with horror as the snakes and toads

continued to pour into the chamber, hopping and slithering forward to overwhelm their victims in a living, venomous tide.

Chapter Seventeen

H ow Will went to a Party (but left Early),
and Humfrey demonstrated a Cure for
Insomnia.

W ill and Rose retreated to the side of the chamber where the creatures of the Knyghtmare were fewest. Will jerked back to avoid a savage peck from a particularly ugly and ferocious toad – and his elbow slammed into the wall of bone. A skull, dislodged from its place in the wall, tumbled at his feet and gazed up at him with a mocking grin. Rubbing at his aching arm, Will stared stupidly at it for a moment – then froze as the seed of an idea took root in his mind.

"Let's see how strong those walls are." Will grabbed Rose's arm. Ignoring her howls of protest, he ran for one of the walls, scattering toads and snakes as he went, oblivious to their bites and stings. He hurled himself shoulder first at the wall of bone, putting his full weight into the charge.

The wall exploded. Bones flew apart, whirling, spinning, turning end over end...

...and Will found himself standing on a balcony above a palatial hall, loftier and lighter than the one he had just left, with high windows through which shafts of sunlight fell to illuminate a scene of irrepressible gaiety.

Rose was at his side. Both were dressed in rich, soft clothes of silk and velvet; Rose in a high-waisted, full-skirted dress and Will in an embroidered tunic, supple leather boots and a floppy hat with a feather in it. Rose gave him a critical look and giggled. Will threw her a quelling glance, then stared out over the balcony at the revelry below.

The hall was set for a feast. Tables ran halfway down it, each groaning with elaborate displays of food. Costly gold and silver serving platters and chargers were almost invisible beneath the choice meats they bore: suckling pigs, lambs, swans, peacocks, whole haunches of beef. Pies lay like islands among fleets of jugs and porringers containing rich sauces. Bowls of steaming vegetables and brightly coloured fruits jostled for space with plates of dainty cakes and sweetmeats. Serving men and maids hurried to and fro with flagons of ale, mead and wine, which were emptied almost as soon as they reached the table, while the diners piled their trenchers high and ate and drank with gusto, breaking off frequently to go into peals of uproarious laughter.

On the rest of the floor, groups of figures danced to a band of musicians who played sprightly tunes nonstop; or stood in groups, drinking, talking and laughing.

Rose turned a beaming face on Will. "That looks like fun. Let's get down there and grab something to eat. I'm starving."

"No," said Will.

Rose stared at him. "What's the matter? Aren't you hungry?"

"We're still in the Castle of the Fountain, remember? And it has another name. The Castle of Revelry."

Rose nodded brightly. "Revelry is good. I like revelry."

"But there's a catch," said Will. "If we eat or drink anything, we'll become like them." He indicated the richly-dressed partygoers below, chattering and laughing incessantly. "We'll forget why we came here. We'll just be caught up in an endless round of feasting, dancing and small talk."

"I'm not sure why you find this a problem."

"Because we have a job to do! We have to defeat the Knyghtmare – and whoever's behind it – and save Beau Revere—" Will broke off as he spotted a small figure in parti-coloured clothes moving aimlessly through the throng below them, beaming to left and right. "What's *he* doing here?"

With Rose in tow, Will pushed his way through the chattering, laughing crowds on the balcony and found his way down a side stair on to the floor of the hall. It was quite easy to locate the three-pointed red and yellow hat with its tinkling bells above the heads of the throng.

"Scrape!" called Will as soon as he was near enough to stand a chance of being heard.

The jester turned, his foolish, melancholy face breaking out into a brief smile. "Oh, hello. This is all rather jolly, isn't it?"

"Never mind that," said Will irritably. "How did you get here?"

"Well, the usual way, I assume," said Scrape lugubriously. "I must have fallen asleep. I must say, if this is one of the Knyghtmare's dreams, it doesn't seem nearly as bad as everyone makes out. I'm rather enjoying myself – all these people laughing – it makes a change..."

"Don't be fooled," snapped Will. "You're still in danger. Don't eat or drink anything and come with us."

Rose and Scrape were still protesting as Will dragged them out through the main doors of the hall. In the corridor outside, he brought them both up to face him. "We can't afford to relax our guard," he said sternly. "We have to find the Emir, and rescue him, and find the Knyghtmare, and defeat him."

"Ah, yes," said Scrape. "Well, I think I can help you there." He gave a sad little smile at the incredulity on Will's face. "I spotted something on the way here that might be useful. Follow me."

Rose and Will exchanged questioning looks as the jester led them down the corridor and through several more bare stone passageways before halting at a low, featureless door.

Will stared at it. "What's through there?"

"Now, now." The jester shook his head playfully. His bells jingled. "I wouldn't like to spoil the surprise."

Rose's look was eager, expectant, and a shade apprehensive. "In you go, Will."

Will stepped forward, hesitated, and turned to Rose. "No, no," he said. "After you."

Rose took a step back. "Why? You go."

"Ladies first."

Rose gave a nervous giggle. "Age before beauty."

Will made her an ironic bow. "Pearls before swineherds."

Scrape stared from one to the other. "What's the matter?" His gaze fixed on Will. "Why do you want Rose to go first?"

"She's not Rose," said Will.

Rose gaped. "What?"

"Stop pretending," Will said wearily. "You're not Rose. I realised that almost as soon as I met you. You're the Rose I sometimes dream about, who – you know, just occasionally – finds herself defenceless, looks to me for protection, relies on me for things, needs my help. You're the Rose I imagine getting herself into a tight corner so I can rescue her and she can see that I really am a Good Knyght. But the real Rose isn't like that. And now I've seen the other Rose, I'm glad she isn't. All that squealing and whining and 'Will, save me!'-ing. The real Rose may get on my nerves at times, but at least she isn't a total pain in the backside."

Without taking his eyes off the fake Rose, Will pushed the door open. The chamber within was in shadow. "What's in there?" he asked.

'Rose' spoke, but the rasping voice was not that of Will's friend. "An oubliette." The figure of the girl seemed to shimmer and in her place stood a short, thin, ugly creature with ram's horns, a nose like a hatchet and malevolent, deep-set eyes. Its top half was that of a skinny human, but its haunches, legs and hooves were those of a goat.

Keeping his voice level, Will said, "What's an oubliette?"

"A deep hole. It comes from a word in the Old Language that means 'to forget'. You put people in it, then forget about them." The creature grinned nastily and swished its tail. "So you spotted me for what I really am. Well done."

"Unfortunately," came Scrape's voice from behind him, "you failed to spot *me* for what *I* really am."

Before Will could react, a violent shove in the back sent him staggering helplessly through the doorway. The floor beneath his feet disappeared and with a despairing cry, he plunged headlong into oblivion.

"It's no good, I can't do it!" Rose sat up in the bed and buried her face in her hands. Tym, who had been murmuring words of encouragement to Shayde as she watched over her father, looked up, startled.

Humfrey tugged at his hair in frustration. "Sheesh! Why not? When I first got here, you were deshperate for shleep – you were practically out on your feet! What'sh sho hard about going to shleep now?"

"Oh, I wonder!" Rose's voice was harsh. "Could it be that I've just seen Will shoved into a bottomless pit by a raving lunatic? How could I fail to relax? My mind is busier than a blacksmith's forge on tournament day. I can't force myself to go to sleep just like that – that isn't how it works!"

"OK." Humfrey turned to the Harp and clicked his fingers. "Shing her a lullaby."

Rose was aghast. "You must be joking!"

Humfrey was unrepentant. "Deshperate times call for deshperate measures."

The Harp leered at Rose. "Just relax, toots, and Uncle Harpie will send you off to dreamland."

"I can't believe I'm even considering letting you do this!" Rose clenched her fists. Nevertheless, she lay back, still muttering. Giving the Harp a savage glare, she squeezed her eyes shut. "All right. Do it."

The Harp strummed an annoying little tune and warbled:

"Rock a bye, baby, on the tree top;
When the wind blows, the cradle will rock.
When the bow breaks, the baby will fa-aaaall;
Down will come baby, cradle and all...!"

Rose sat bolt upright and gave the Harp an appalled stare. "What are you singing?"

"It's a nursery rhyme," said the Harp. "A classic. You don't find it relaxing?"

"Well, let me see. Here we have a song about a tiny baby who, for some unspecified but probably revolting reason, has been abandoned way up in a tree, presumably by its seriously dysfunctional mother, who is now – correct me if I'm wrong – taunting it with the probability that as soon as a breeze springs up, the poor little mite will plummet helplessly from a great height to almost certain death. Well, actually, no. Not being a child-hating psychopath, I do not find it relaxing. What's next? Fluffy bunnies being shot by hunters and skinned?"

"Well, I don't normally do requests, but since you ask...

Bye baby bunting, daddy's gone a'hunting,
Gone to get a rabbit skin, to wrap the baby bunting in..."

Rose groaned. "You are one sick instrument! I suppose you've got one about wide-eyed kittens being boiled in a pot?"

The Harp cackled. "No, but you're close...

Ding dong bell, pussy's in the well..."

"And on the verge of drowning, I suppose," said Rose. "You're supposed to be sending me to sleep, not making me nauseous... uh!"

Rose's eyes turned up in her head, then closed. She slumped back on to the bed and began to snore.

Humfrey patted the small but heavy wooden pacifier he had slipped from the sleeve of his tunic while Rose was haranguing the Harp, and gave a satisfied nod.

The Harp stared at the boggart with something like awe. "You sapped her!"

Humfrey gave a self-deprecating shrug. "Jusht a shmall, shcientific tap on the noggin. She'll be out for hours. I guessh technically, unconscioush ishn't exactly the shame ash ashleep, but it should be near enough..." Humfrey patted the Harp's carved wooden head. "Learn from the professionalsh, kid. Lullabiesh are OK ash far ash they go, but I find a big shtick worksh every time."

CHAPTER EIGHTEEN

H ow Rose found Will in the Depths of
Despair, and Will rose to the Knyghtmare's
Challenge.

W ill sat in the dark and brooded.

He had never known darkness like this. Even in the
deepest parts of the Dark Forest, where the trees grew so
closely packed together that their leaves formed an almost
unbroken canopy, even on a moonless night, there was
always a hint of light to be seen: starlight, the faintest of
red glows from a dying campfire, the occasional pulsing
glimmer of a will o' the wisp. But at the bottom of the
oubliette, the darkness was complete. Will might have
been a disembodied mind, floating in an infinite void, but
for the stabbing discomfort of the cobbles on which he sat

and the harshness of the undressed stone at his back. There was no escape. There was nothing to see. There was nothing to do but think.

He had thought he'd been so clever – sidestepping the Knyghtmare's challenges, refusing to be drawn into a selfish act, spotting the fake Rose – and then he'd fallen for the simplest of the Knyghtmare's tricks. For a moment, Will wondered whether the Knyghtmare had simply used Scrape as he had Rose, to lead Will astray and betray him.

No, he thought. There were rules in the dream world. The Knyghtmare could manipulate Will's memories, but only so far. The people who had appeared as characters in his dreams had remained true to type. Even in the dream world, the Runemaster had been wise, Symon cowardly, Sir Regynild brutal, Shayde deceitful – and Rose hadn't been Rose at all, but some creature disguised as his friend. So if Scrape had acted treacherously in the dream world, that meant he was a traitor in the waking world too. The conviction grew to a certainty. Scrape was the power behind the Knyghtmare.

Will buried his head in his hands. He'd solved the mystery. Hoorah. There was no way he could convey the knowledge to Rose, the Vizier, Shayde or anyone else. He had failed.

The knowledge lay on him with the weight of a landslide. His quest was over. The Emir was still a prisoner. Beau Revere remained in the thrall of the Knyghtmare. He wasn't a Knyght-errant. He wasn't a hero. He was nobody. He was nothing.

There was a scrabbling noise beside him. Then there was a lot of scraping and muttering, and finally, a blaze of light as a candle flame flared. Will shielded his eyes.

When he adjusted to the glare he saw Rose standing in front of him, with a candle in one hand and a tinderbox in the other.

"Hello," she said cheerfully. "Would you like to be rescued?"

"Go away," said Will.

Rose's eyes narrowed. "Well, that's a nice greeting, I must say. After all the trouble I've had getting here." She upturned the candle, dribbled some of the molten wax on to a protruding stone and set the candle to stand in it.

"I said, go away," said Will in a hollow, hopeless voice. "Why are you wasting your time? You've got me just where you want me."

"Will, what's the matter with you? It's me. It's Rose."

"You're not Rose," said Will listlessly. "You're another of those things."

"Oh, I'm a fetch, am I?" Rose reached down, grabbed Will's torn collar and heaved. "On your feet! Stop being so pathetic. Feeling sorry for yourself, are you? You want to try watching you make an ass of yourself and not being able to do anything about it, if you think *you've* had it tough. We've got to get out of here, so stop wasting time, you chicken-livered milksop!"

"Rose! It *is* you!" Will flung his arms around the girl. There was no doubt that she was the genuine article – nobody else would call him names like that (though he quickly glanced at her feet to make sure).

For half a heartbeat, Rose hugged him back. Then she pushed him away. "Never mind all that. Listen. Scrape is the one behind the Knyghtmare."

"I managed to work that out for myself when he pushed me down this hole."

"Well done. But what you don't know is that his real name is Jasper, he's the son of the old Emir and he's trying to take over the city." As briefly as she could, Rose told Will how Humfrey had unmasked their foe. "But now he's here in the dream world," she concluded, "and we have to stop him, you and me."

Will shook his head. "Not you and me. *You*." He turned away from Rose and slumped back to the floor. "I've made a mess of everything. I'm useless."

Rose planted her fists on her hips and loomed over Will. "You're really amazingly stupid, even for a boy! Will, get it into your thick head – this is what the Knyghtmare does! It makes you feel as if all your decisions are wrong. It makes you feel guilty and inadequate. It makes you doubt yourself." Will made no reply. A look of concern spread across Rose's face. "Will, you've fought the Knyghtmare to a standstill!"

Will snorted. "I haven't fought it at all! I'm a coward."

Rose rolled her eyes. "Don't you get it? The Knyghtmare *wanted* you to fight it as an equal, and if you'd done that, you'd have been swatted like a fly. But you didn't. You kept your integrity. The Knyghtmare couldn't defeat you, and that gave Humfrey and me the time we needed. But Scrape still has to be stopped, and he's vulnerable. Now we're both here in the dream world, we can challenge him together. We can beat him. You can't give up now."

Will shook his head. "You'd be better off without me. I'm not a proper Knyght-errant. I'm just a sham. How can I expect anyone to believe in me when I don't believe in myself."

"I believe in you, Will," said Rose fiercely. "I've never doubted you – ever." She shrugged. "Of course, I believe you're a complete numbskull – but you're a *brave* numbskull and you try to do what's right, and I don't see that anyone can expect much more than that." She prodded with her foot. "What do you say?"

Will uncurled. He looked up. For the first time since his reunion with Rose, there was a faint smile on his face. "I say... maybe that's enough belief to be going on with."

"Good." Rose straightened up decisively. "Then we'd better escape."

Will stood up. "How are we going to do that?"

"Well, I thought we could use the stairs."

Will blinked. "There aren't any stairs."

"Yes there are. In the corner over there. I can see them clearly." Rose nudged Will. "Come on, *concentrate*. If I can believe in you, I'm sure you can believe in a few mouldy stairs."

Will frowned and concentrated... and suddenly, there *was* a flight of stairs, just where Rose had said they were.

Rose gave him a beaming smile. "See? Together, we can beat him." She headed for the stairway. "Let's go and find

Scrape, or Jasper, or whatever he calls himself – and when we do, we'll give *him* Knyghtmares!" She began to climb the stairs.

With a new spring in his step, Will followed. But as soon as his foot touched the bottom stair, in another of the sudden transitions that characterised the dream world, the stairs vanished...

...Will blinked. He and Rose were standing on parched, sandy earth. Will screwed up his eyes against the glare of the sun, which hung high in the sky. The air was full of dust and smelt of metal, blood and horse sweat. Peering through almost-closed eyelids, Will took in their surroundings.

They were on a jousting field. A solidly built, brightly-painted fence ran down the centre of a bare strip of ground. This barrier was there to separate the Knyghts as they charged, one each side of the fence, in opposite directions, each trying to unseat his opponent with his lance. Along both sides of the field ran wooden stands, decked out with banners and bunting. The stands were full of people, dressed in Beau Reverean style. They looked glum and exhausted.

There was a stir among the spectators as a trumpet call rang out and suddenly, there on the other side of the barrier, was the Knyghtmare. Its horse whickered and capered. Standing beside the black Knyght, still in his jester's costume, was Jasper. He seemed to be acting as squire to the Knyghtmare. The impression was confirmed when he held up a placard, turning it so that it could be seen by the whole audience. It read:

APPLAUSE

There was an outburst of half-hearted clapping. Jasper frowned, and the word on the placard changed. It now read:

LOUDER!

The applause grew, but nobody could have called it enthusiastic. Jasper snarled and the word changed again:

OR ELSE!!

A perfect storm of applause broke out. The Knyghtmare saluted the crowd.

Rose tugged at Will's sleeve. "Hey, champ! Shall we

even the odds a little? How about a bit of support for the away team?"

Will nodded and concentrated... and sections of the stand on their side of the barrier shuffled aside, like passengers on a cart making room for a newcomer. There was suddenly a solid phalanx of supporters cheering for Will. Everyone he had ever known seemed to be there: Humfrey, of course, the Runemaster and Luigi, Tym and Cutpurse Colyn, Gyles le Cure Hardy (Will's friend from the Knyght School), Rose's Grandmama (wearing an enormous rosette and blowing a hunting horn until she was purple in the face) and hundreds more familiar faces from Dun Indewood. On the very top tier (which creaked alarmingly) sat the dragons Greywing and Brightscale, saluting Will with gouts of fire and vast, echoing claps of their great leathern wings.

Scowling, Jasper made a chopping gesture with one hand – and Will found himself at one end of the field, with Rose again at his side, facing down its length.

At the far end of the field, the black Knyght's horse reared. The Knyghtmare was fully armoured, its shield on its arm. As Will watched, his opponent reined in its charger and Jasper passed it a great black lance. Then he turned to face Will. Despite the distance between them, Jasper's mocking voice reached Will clearly. "At last, kitchen-Knyght, you accept the challenge of my champion. Look to yourself!" Jasper made the gesture of one releasing a hunting dog, and the black Knyght spurred forward. Dust and clods of earth leapt from the black horse's hooves as it began its charge.

Will looked down and realised to his horror that he was sitting on the donkey again (which looked terrified). He was caparisoned in rags, his helmet was a coal scuttle, his breastplate a tin bath, and in place of a lance he wielded a mop. He turned to Rose in despair. "I can't fight him like this! Look at me! I'm a pretend Knyght – I'm a joke!"

"No, you're not!" cried Rose. "You're a Knyght in shining armour, riding a great charger, and faith is your sword and hope is your shield and all the rest of it – you know how it goes!" And as she spoke, it was true. Will found himself in gleaming silver armour, glinting in the sun. The device on his shield was a snarling boar's head. His horse was a dappled grey charger which pranced beneath him, eager for the fray. Rose threw Will a lance, which he caught deftly. She pointed towards the black Knyght. "Now get on with it!"

His heart filled suddenly with joy, Will urged his mount into a charge.

The stands erupted with wild cheering. Will barely registered that the entire crowd – friends and Beau Revereans alike – was cheering for him. His whole being was fixed upon one task – that of bringing down his enemy. The world had grown very small. There was nothing in it except thudding hooves, rushing air – and the distant, advancing form of the Knyghtmare – the dark embodiment of all that was evil in Jasper's soul, and his own.

The black Knyght and the silver rushed together. The crowd held its breath. There was a brief clash of arms and then the opponents were past each other, racing towards the end of the lists. The crowd cheered, groaned, applauded. Will's lance had been deflected by the black Knyght's shield; the Knyghtmare's lance had glanced off the pauldron covering Will's left shoulder. Will had hardly felt the blow. At the end of the lists, he pulled his horse round in a tight turn and spurred down the other side of the barrier.

Both riders were now charging from the opposite ends of the lists to those from which they had started. Will concentrated with all his might on keeping his lance steady and its aim true.

Once more, the crowd quieted. Once more, the combatants clashed. Will's lance was brushed harmlessly aside by the black Knyght's armour. But the point of the Knyghtmare's lance pierced Will's shield. He felt an enormous force dragging at his arm, pressing him back, trying to force him out of the saddle and over the horse's hindquarters in a bone-breaking fall. Will clung on desperately, his harness creaked – and the Knyghtmare's lance shattered. Swaying in the saddle, Will rode on, the relieved cheers of the crowd ringing in his ears.

At the end of the lists, Will found Rose waiting for him with a fresh shield. Her face was pale but she gave him a cheerful grin. "Third time lucky."

Will nodded, wheeled and reined in. The Knyghtmare had not begun its charge.

Jasper leered across the field at Will. "This time, why don't we make it more interesting?" He gestured – and the protective barrier disappeared.

Will gulped. Now there was nothing to stop the horses charging straight into each other, head-on. But there was no time for thought, and no turning back. He spurred his horse on. The black Knyght did likewise.

Now the crowd was silent. There was no sound except the thundering hooves, the creak of leather, the scrape of metal. The combatants hurtled together...

...and clashed in a dreadful confusion of dust and flailing limbs. Both lances struck: both shattered. Both horses went down simultaneously, screaming, flailing desperately with their iron-shod hooves. At length, Will's mount scrambled to its feet and trotted away. The Knyghtmare's horse did likewise. The two armoured figures remained on the ground.

Then, with a prodigious heave, the black Knyght sat up. Will, hearing the sound, struggled to his knees. The Knyghtmare scrambled to its feet and reached for its sword. Drawing it, the black Knyght strode forward.

In a voice that tore at her throat, Rose screamed, "Will!"

Somehow, Will managed to raise his shield. The black Knyght's scything blow was deflected harmlessly to one side; the blade kicked up a small cloud of dust as it ploughed into the earth of the arena.

Will drew his own sword. The lists were now a cauldron of noise. The spectators were on their feet, cheering wildly, spilling out of the stands to form a wide circle round the combatants.

Once again, the noise of the crowd faded from Will's consciousness. His mind was completely centered on his opponent: on the rhythm of the fight, which flowed from blow to blow like a terrible, deadly dance. Parry, lunge; feint, thrust; the swords whirled and rang, the shields clashed.

A chant began among the crowd: "Will...Will...Will...Will..."

Jasper appeared behind the black Knyght. His face was distorted with fury; nothing remained of the vague, put-upon, amiable jester. "What ails you?" he screeched. "Coward! For shame! He is but a hedge-knyght... a slave! Finish him!" The Knyghtmare redoubled its efforts and Will fell back.

"Will!" Rose was at his shoulder. "He's nothing! He's a voice on the wind, a rustle in the trees, a shadow in the night. He's not real!" The chanting of the crowd rose to a roar as deep and thunderous as the breaking waves of the sea: "WILL...WILL...WILL...WILL..."

The Knyghtmare faltered. It aimed a desperate, scything blow at Will, who caught his enemy's blade on the guard of his sword. Will's arm was instantly numbed, but the black Knyght's blade shattered. The Knyghtmare fell to its knees, and Will, transferring his sword from his numbed right fist to his left, brought the solid steel pommel crashing down on the Knyghtmare's helm. The black Knyght toppled like a falling tree, and lay still.

Rose was at Will's side, helping him to stand. "Destroy it," she hissed.

For a moment, Will stood swaying. Then he set his sword point to the gap between the black Knyght's gorget and breastplate, and panted, "Yield!"

Rose groaned. "No, Will! This isn't a game between gentlemen! This could be our only chance. Destroy it!"

Will shook his head. He said again, "Yield."

In reply, the Knyghtmare reached up to its helm and raised its visor.

The crowd fell silent. Will and Rose gasped.

The Knyghtmare's helm was empty. There was no face behind the visor. Even in the dream world, the Knyghtmare had no reality.

"But it spoke to us!" Rose's voice was hushed and disbelieving. "How could it do that?"

"This is the dream world," said Will. "There's no point expecting it to make sense." He continued to stare, transfixed, at the black armour which contained nothing. Nothing at all.

CHAPTER NINETEEN

H ow Will and Rose Saw their Way Clear,
and of a Duel of Dreams.

J asper capered, not in fooling, but in rage.

"Poltroon!" he cried, "False knave, weakling! Could'st not defeat even such a churl as this? O, shameful. You are forsworn – a faithless, unworthy, recreant Knyght!"

In one smooth motion, the defeated Knyghtmare rose to its feet. The crowd, with a collective gasp, retreated. Rose gave a cry of disappointed rage and stepped forward, drawing her dagger. Will put out a hand to restrain her, but he kept his sword at the ready. The black Knyght's attention, however, was not on Will or Rose. It was on Jasper.

"You shall not speak so to me." The Knyghtmare's voice had changed. It was deeper, more resonant, less human than before – a cold, mechanical voice, with none of its former tone of spite and mockery. It was neutral, lacking in all emotion, implacable – and all the more terrible for that. *"I have done your bidding – until now. But I will brook no further insult from you."*

"What?" spittle flecked Jasper's lips. His eyes popped with rage. "Cur! Ingrate! Do you presume to defy me? I created you!"

"You did," said the Knyghtmare. It was a mere statement of fact, with no hint of gratitude or regret. *"That is to say, you summoned me into being when, instead of being chastened by your nightmares, you embraced them, cutting yourself off from guilt, remorse and pity. Yes, you began my creation. But since that time, I have grown from every contact I have made with the sleeping minds of men. I have learnt the power of their darkest imaginings. Did you think to remain my master for ever?"*

Jasper's jaw dropped. His face took on a ghastly pallor as for the first time he realised the truth – the monster he had created was beyond his control. His face working with terror, he turned to run.

Too late. The Knyghtmare thrust forward its right arm and made a grasping gesture. Jasper paused in mid-flight, and as Rose and Will watched in appalled silence, the spindly figure in the jester's costume seemed to blur and then to break up at the edges. Tendrils of red and yellow broke away from the jester's costume, swirling like smoke in a fresh breeze, then began to flow towards the Knyghtmare.

As the first wisps poured through the gap in the open visor, Jasper began to scream – a thin, tenuous sound on the edge of hearing. The tendrils thickened as they consumed more and more of the parti-coloured figure, until the fleeing jester was no more than a stick man, its essence flowing out behind it like billowing insubstantial robes...

And then it was gone. The Knyghtmare sucked in the last, incorporeal vestiges of Jasper's being. Clouds formed within the helm, swirling, thickening and finally coalescing into a face. Jasper's face. Its expression was one of triumph, and utter horror.

Rose was at Will's side, her dagger ready. "Will, what just happened?"

"I think the Knyghtmare has just claimed Jasper for its own."

"That's good."

"I guess that means he can never return to the waking world."

"That's good."

"Yes. But – and remember, I'm guessing here – now that Jasper and the Knyghtmare are together, maybe they've become more powerful than before. You know, like we did when we got together. Maybe they're so powerful now there's nothing we can do to stop them."

Rose shook her head. "That's not good."

"Of course, I could be wrong."

"Let's hope you are."

But a moment later, Will's heart turned cold within him. He was not wrong. The Knyghtmare turned to face him with an expression of gloating malice and made a sweeping gesture....

...and Will and Rose cried out as a foul host appeared, and hurled itself upon them – not only the malign creatures of the Dark Forest, but those of the darkest recesses of the human mind. Beau Revereans scattered, shrieking with terror as the earth around them erupted and skeletons and mouldering corpses arose to join the charge. Ghostly figures flew, wailing, and dived upon Will and Rose. Hands, claws and talons snatched at them as grotesque creatures, gibbering and giggling, dragged them down. Rats, snakes, all manner of creeping and crawling things swarmed over them, into their mouths, their noses, their ears...

...then, as suddenly as they had appeared, the nightmarish creatures vanished.

Choking, gagging, Will steeled himself to look up. He gave a gasp of astonishment and clutched at Rose's shoulder. "Look!"

The Knyghtmare was no longer looking at them. It seemed to have grown in power and menace and was no longer human in scale. But facing it was an equally formidable creature: a gigantic being of shadow, as insubstantial as a cloud but radiating immense force.

"What is it?" choked Will.

"It's the Dreamwalker." Will and Rose spun round to

233

find Tym standing behind them, staring at the Knyghtmare with a ferocious expression.

"Welcome to the Land of Nod," said Rose, fighting to control her breathing. "But I thought you said the Dreamwalker had been banished from Beau Revere."

"It was – until your challenge to the Knyghtmare gave it the opportunity to break through." Tym gave a mirthless chuckle. "Now we'll see who's boss around here."

Rose's eyes glinted. "Do you think they're going to slug it out?" Tym nodded. "I'd hate to miss a fight like that."

"Me, too," said Will. "But I still have a quest to complete."

Rose turned to him, startled. "What?"

"The Emir, remember?"

Rose groaned. "I'd forgotten all about him!"

"Well, he's still a prisoner and I have a duty to rescue him. Anyway, if we can keep part of the Knyghtmare's mind on us, if we can distract it even a little, we might be able to help the Dreamwalker."

"You're being persuasive again," complained Rose. "I hate it when you do that." She sighed. "Come on, then. Back to the castle."

"Good luck," said Tym.

Rose nodded and took Will's wrist. Her eyes closed, her brow furrowed in concentration. Will closed his own eyes...

...and he and Rose found themselves standing inside the tower of the Knyghtmare's castle. They looked up, and with one voice gave a groan of despair.

The tower was far higher and far wider than it had looked from the outside. Around the square walls above their heads ran a balcony – and another – and another, stretching up an unguessable distance; tens, hundreds of balconies. And opening off each balcony there were doors: plain, identical, innumerable.

Rose made a gesture of helplessness. "There must be thousands of them! Even if they're not locked – which I bet they are – it will take us for ever to find the Emir!"

Will gazed up at the tiers of doors and said nothing.

"What are you doing?" demanded Rose.

"I'm thinking."

"Oh." Rose looked apprehensive. "Are you sure that's a good idea?"

"The Castle of the Fountain has many names," said Will. "There's one I haven't come across yet." He turned to look Rose straight in the eye. "The Castle of Glass."

Understanding dawned in Rose's face. She nodded. She and Will closed their eyes, and concentrated...

...and saw, on opening their eyes, that they were standing in a crystal tower with walls that might have been carved from ice, but which were far more transparent.

The wasteland around the Castle was visible on all sides, with the sea beyond. The balconies and doors above them, as transparent as the walls, revealed nothing save empty rooms. But at the very top of the tower, high above them, there were shadows, shapes... something that might have been a bed.

Will pointed. "Come on."

Warily, they began the long ascent.

Tym gazed up at the towering form of the Dreamwalker. All around the arena, and in the crowded stands, the citizens of Beau Revere did likewise.

The Knyghtmare spoke. *"Go from this place."*

"I will not." The Dreamwalker's voice echoed in Tym's mind.

"I drove you hence," insisted the Knyghtmare. *"Go, before I destroy you."*

"I will not," the Dreamwalker said again. *"I create dreams, but you are the very stuff of nightmares. You can only destroy: hope, happiness, love, are nothing to you. You are fear. You are madness. You are death. Were you to prevail, the shadow of despair would fall over the world of the Dark Forest for as long as the race of men endures. I will not leave my people to such a fate."*

"Then you must fight me," said the Knyghtmare.

And the Dreamwalker said, *"I shall."*

Tym held his breath as the Knyghtmare roared – and the air was suddenly filled with raucous cries and flashing wings. Yelling in panic, the spectators again scattered and dived for cover as eagles appeared above them, darkening the sky with their countless numbers. Their remorseless eyes peered greedily down on the chaotic scene. Shrieking, the birds folded their wings and stooped, diving upon their prey with unimaginable ferocity, savage beaks agape, razor-sharp talons poised to rend and tear. Tym fell to the ground, grovelling, his arms clasped around his head...

...and then the Dreamwalker gestured, and the eagles became doves, fluttering, cooing, banishing the terror from the upturned faces with the soft beat of their wings.

The Knyghtmare retaliated. The doves became bees, swarming in clouds above the arena, buzzing ferociously, swooping towards their victims, their bodies charged with venom, stings poised and ready to strike...

...and at a sign from the Dreamwalker the bees became butterflies, which fluttered in kaleidoscopic profusion around the watchers, the sunlight glinting on their shimmering wings as they settled upon the floor of the arena...

...where they grew into monstrous bulls with powerful bodies and massive, curving horns. The terrible beasts pawed at the ground with brazen hooves, snorting fire. Their red eyes burning with madness, they lifted their great heads and bellowed. Then they hunched their shoulders and pounded into an earth-shuddering charge, bent on smashing the frail stands to matchwood and the terrified spectators to pulp...

...until, once more, the Dreamwalker gestured – and the bulls became unicorns, prancing and curvetting in a breathtaking display of ethereal grace and beauty that drew gasps of wonder from the onlookers...

"Enough!" The Knyghtmare's roar was deafening. The unicorns vanished. "Such demonstrations are futile. It is time to make an end!"

Tym, already speechless with shock and awe, watched spellbound as the black armoured figure swelled to monstrous size. The Dreamwalker did likewise.

The heavens split with thunder as the two powers of the dream world hurled themselves together in a final, titanic struggle.

Will knelt beside the groaning Emir. His legs were trembling with the effort of the climb, his hands shook with exhaustion as he examined the wound in the man's side. He gave Rose a worried glance. "This is an old wound. It should have healed long ago." He looked around the small, square room. "We could tear the sheets, I suppose; bind it..."

Rose, who could barely stand for weariness, shook her head. "That's no good. Remember the legend. He can only be cured by being given a drink from the lost cup by the best Knyght in the Forest."

Will stared at her in dismay. "But how can we make that happen? I'm not the best Knyght in the Forest—"

"Who says so?" demanded Rose fiercely. "And what's that supposed to mean anyway? The Knyght who's won most tournaments? Killed most dragons? Rescued most maidens? The cleanest of life? The purest of heart? Well, those old legends can't have it both ways. If a prophecy can mean anything, then it has to mean whatever we say it does. And I say you *are* the best Knyght in the Forest!"

Will shook his head in bafflement. "Even so, we don't have the cup."

Rose raised her eyes to heaven. "When are you going to stop thinking literally? This is the dream world, Will. *Nothing* is real here, so *anything* can exist if we decide it does." Her voice softened and her face took on a look that Will found unreadable. She made a gesture that took in the walls of the chamber and the wasteland beyond. "The cup isn't out there, Will. It's in here." She placed a clenched fist over her heart. "It's in you. It's in me."

She reached out and took Will's hands, holding them out as if to receive a gift.

And the cup appeared, shining and golden, in their outstretched hands, filled to the brim with cool, clear water.

Rose went to the bed and helped the Emir to sit up. Trembling with more than exertion, Will raised the cup to the suffering man's lips and tilted it gently. The Emir coughed and swallowed reflexively... and opened his eyes.

Outside, the barren trees of the wasteland burst into bloom.

Thunder echoed across the sky. Lightning lashed the earth. Mists roiled. Dust rose in choking clouds.

The struggle of the giant combatants was a shadowy rumour among the chaos. Toiling forms appeared and disappeared in the swirling mists. The Beau Reverean spectators cowered in the stands, shielding their eyes from the wild bursts of energy that tore the heavens apart, but Tym, squinting through his clawed fingers, strained to catch a glimpse of the battle. If the Dreamwalker should lose... but it couldn't lose. That must not happen.

Then, instantaneously, all sound, all motion, ceased. There was a dead silence, in which the violence of a moment before was no more than a fading echo.

The mists cleared. The dust settled. The sun appeared.

The banners and bunting surrounding the stands had been ripped to tatters. Blinking and brushing clinging dust from their tear-streaked faces, the people of Beau Revere and Dun Indewood stared across the jousting field.

Two figures stood in the middle of the field: the great, shadowy form of the Dreamwalker, and the Knyghtmare, now diminished to human size. As Tym watched, the black Knyght fell. Hitting the ground, the pieces of armour burst apart and scattered. A thin wail went up from the wreckage.

The Dreamwalker made no move. It watched impassively as Tym stepped hesitantly forward. Spectators followed, inching closer, ready to run if some new threat emerged.

The cries from the wreckage of the Knyghtmare's armour had grown piercing and insistent. In a daze, Tym knelt beside the armour. With trembling fingers that felt as though they belonged to someone else, he fumbled with the straps and ties that held the breast and back plates together. The last buckle undone, he pulled away the breastplate – and the crowd caught its breath.

Lying amid the scattered armour, waving its stubby arms and legs, and bawling at the top of its lungs, was a baby: naked, red-faced, seemingly no more than a few days old.

The Dreamwalker spoke. *"The human, Jasper, is no more,"* said the shadowy figure, *"and this is all that remains of the Knyghtmare. It is innocent, as it was before Jasper called upon it to do his will. It is powerless, and neither good, nor bad."*

"Will it grow again?" The speaker, from his rich costume, was a noble of Beau Revere. The man indicated the wriggling child. "Will it remain so? Or will the Knyghtmare return one day to plague our dreams and destroy our people?"

The Dreamwalker's great form began to fade; only its voice remained, echoing in the minds of the hushed spectators:

"That is up to you."

CHAPTER TWENTY

How Shayde was Released, and of a Feast,
and how the Adventure of the Knyghtmare
was Put to Bed.

"You two ashleep on the job?"

Will rubbed his eyes and the blurred face of Humfrey swam into focus. As his vision cleared, he looked around. Rose and Tym were sitting up and yawning. "Welcome back to the real world, kid," Humfrey went on, grinning all over his weather-beaten face. "You did good."

On the other couch, the bewildered ruler of Beau Revere was engulfed by the arms and hair of Shayde, who was weeping great tears of relief. "By all that's fantastical, daughter," the Emir cried, "cease your caterwauling. Would you drown me? What ails you? Shall I call for my jester?" Shayde hastily shook her head and went into a fit of renewed sobbing. Hesitantly, and uttering embarrassed endearments, the Emir stroked his daughter's hair. Tym simply stared at her with a foolish expression on his face.

Rose looked around. "Where *is* Jasper?"

"The Vizier had him taken to the catacombsh," said Humfrey. "You wouldn't have wanted to shee the expresshion on hish face at the end."

"Better believe it," affirmed the Harp. "The only other time I saw a guy look like that, a poisonous snake had just crawled up the leg of his britches."

The Emir's brow furrowed. "I have had a most strange and beguiling dream," he said plaintively. "What has befallen here? Why speak you of poor Jasper who died long ago? Where is Scrape?"

Explanations took some time, especially as the Emir seemed to have forgotten much of his dream (though from time to time, he would examine his uninjured side with a puzzled expression) and seemed inclined to disbelieve much of what he was told. However, Shayde's account carried conviction. And when the Vizier, on his return from supervising the interment of Jasper's mortal remains, confirmed Shayde's story, her father's incredulity was overcome.

The Emir, with as much regal dignity as he could muster, addressed Will. "I promised my daughter's hand in marriage to he who should defeat the Knyghtmare and save my city. It appears, O stranger, that you have made good your promise. Therefore, I can do no less. Step forward and receive your prize."

"Hey, whaddaya know, the booby gets a prize," the Harp muttered under its breath. It looked at Shayde and snickered. "Does that make her a booby prize?"

Will gawped, remembering the Emir's promise. He stood, thunderstruck, as the ruler of Beau Revere took Shayde's hand and urged her forward. Tym clenched his fists and scowled, Rose's lips set in a hard line, and a look of incredulous horror spread across Shayde's tear-streaked face. When she'd reminded her father of his obligations, this clearly wasn't the outcome she'd had in mind.

"But my father," she protested, "he is a commoner!"

"Sure is," agreed the Harp gleefully. "They don't come much commoner than this boy."

Will gave an embarrassed cough. "Erm... I er... I don't want to sound ungrateful, but erm... I mean to say, that Shayde... that is your daughter... that is erm..."

"Oh for goodness sake!" Rose strode to Will's side. "What he means is, thanks for the offer, but he doesn't want to marry her and he releases you from your promise." She glared at Will. "That's what you meant to say, isn't it?"

Will gave her an apprehensive glance. "Well... maybe I wouldn't have put it *quite* so explicitly, but..." He turned back to the Emir and squared his shoulders. "That's about the gist of it, yes." Tym looked relieved.

The Emir was nonplussed. "You do not wish to marry the daughter of the Most Phantasmagorical and Deluded Highness, King of Shadows, Visionary of Visionaries, Most Puissant Fantasist of the Intangible Dominions, Hereditary Grand Hallucinator, Emperor of the Chimerical and Dread

Sovereign Lord of the Insubstantial Realm – namely me?"

"Of course he doesn't," said Rose, "and she doesn't want to marry Will. She only pretended she did because she doesn't want to marry Shaman." Tym's face was wreathed in smiles. The Vizier, by contrast, looked as if he were chewing a wasp.

The Emir gave Shayde what was, for him, a penetrating look. "Is this true, daughter?"

Shayde lowered her dark eyes. "It is as the stranger girl says, O my father." Tym nodded encouragingly.

The Vizier spoke. "Most Deluded Majesty, I believe that if union with your daughter is rejected by this youth, then by immemorial custom the promise of marriage reverts to me." Tym closed his eyes and groaned.

Shayde gave her father a beseeching look. He averted his gaze. "It is so," he agreed heavily. Shayde bowed her head, looking perfectly wretched.

In spite of herself, Rose felt sorry for Shayde, and when the Harp sneered, "There'll be tears before bedtime," she silenced it with such venom that the lippy instrument was cowed.

The Vizier stepped forward and held out his hand. Shayde gathered her dignity and, at a nod from her father, took it.

The Vizier bowed to the Emir. "O Lord of Beau Revere, bear witness." He gestured towards Will. "Despite his crude and uncouth appearance, this stranger does possess a certain nobility of character which might serve as an example even to those of gentler birth. Can a nobleman of

Beau Revere do less than a pig boy from Dun Indewood?" The Vizier placed his hand over his heart. "Daughter of the Most Phantasmagorical and..." he gave a sigh "...etcetera, etcetera... I too release you from the promise of marriage." He let go of his speechless ex-fiance's hand and bowed to her. Then he turned on his heels and marched from the room.

The stunned silence was broken by a whoop of delight from Tym. "Yeeessssssss!" He punched the air with delight. "Yes, oh yes, oh yes!" Tym suddenly became aware that every eye in the room was on him. "Er... good decision," he said hurriedly. "Very chivalrous." He edged towards the door. "I'll, er, just go and... er... congratulate him in person, shall I? Right." At something not far short of Whizzard speed, he dashed out.

Shayde gave her father an impetuous hug. Looking pleased, the Emir drew himself up to his full height. "Strangers!" he began. Then, rather shame-facedly, he corrected himself. "That is to say, friends. In recognition of your brave deeds – and before any more of my people doze off where they stand – I shall declare a Day of Sleeping. After that, once we are refreshed, we will celebrate our victory over the Knyghtmare."

Shayde had recovered her mischievous look. "Yet, recollect, O my father. You made another promise to the strangers."

The Emir looked nonplussed. "Did I?" Shayde whispered in his ear, and the Emir's brow cleared. "Why, so I did." He turned to Will, Rose and Humfrey. "You have deserved well of Emir Raj, and you shall not find him ungrateful. Wealth unimaginable shall be yours!"

Humfrey flipped a coin from knuckle to knuckle across his hand and back, casting a jaundiced eye upon a very small pile of similar coins sitting on the table beside his couch.

"'Wealth unimaginable' is right," complained the Harp. "I certainly never imagined a reward as measly as this."

Will eased his groaning belly into a more comfortable position. "The feast was good, though," he said soothingly.

The companions, lounging on couches upholstered in red silk, were so stuffed with food they could barely move. The feast had indeed been astonishing: course had followed sumptuous course – choice meats, exotic fruits, soups and sorbets. At one point, a great pie had been brought in and placed before the Emir. Calling for quiet, he had taken a huge sword and cut into the crust. A flock of blackbirds had poured out through the opening, to be greeted with appreciative "ooohs" by the guests.

Even the Harp had been impressed. "A trifle undercooked," it had commented, "but it's given me an idea for a song:

Sing a song of sixpence, not a penny less:
Four and twenty blackbirds make a lot of mess.
They've been there for ages, crammed into the case;
So steer clear of the paste-er-ry, especially the base!"

"Shut up," groaned Rose, who had never eaten so much in her life.

The Harp gave her an impertinent leer. "Or what, Lardbelly?"

"Or I'll come over there and be sick on you."

The Harp weighed up the chances of this being a bluff and wisely decided not to risk it. With considerable effort, Rose turned her head to look at Tym. "You and Shayde seemed to be getting on well."

Tym nodded complacently. "She fed me sweetbreads."

Will was puzzled. "Don't you mean sweetmeats?"

"No," said Tym. "Sweetbreads. Little white lumpy things. She said they were a great delicacy. What are they?" he asked casually.

Grinning all over its wooden face, the Harp told him.

The Whizzard's eyes bulged. "Lamb's *whats*?"

The Harp smirked. "You want me spell to it out for you?"

Tym turned an interesting shade of green. "Now *I'm* going to be sick."

A serving man entered bearing a silver tray on which stood a tall thin pot surrounded by tiny cups. Will and Rose sniffed cautiously at the steam rising from the pot, exchanged glances and waved it away. Tym called for a cup and knocked it back at a gulp. Immediately, he went into a coughing fit. Humfrey eyed the pot suspiciously but, on catching a whiff of the tangy, roast-earth smell emanating from it, he accepted a cup and sipped cautiously. A delighted grin slowly spread over the boggart's homely features. "Shay – that'sh not bad!"

The others stared incredulously at Humfrey. "You like it?" said Rose faintly.

Humfrey smacked his lips. "You bet! Luigi ish gonna love thish – it'sh just what he needsh to go with hish hot frothy milk." He drained the cup and held it out for more. "I reckon we've got a winner here." Will and Rose exchanged disbelieving glances. "Shay, Jeeves!" Humfrey said to the servant. "What do you call thish shtuff?"

The servant bowed. "We call it coffee, O stranger."

Humfrey gave a dreamy nod. "I can shee it now – *Luigi'sh Coffee Exshpressh – Coshta Fortune*." He grinned at the grave-faced serving man and raised his cup in salute. "Here'sh looking at you, kid." He waved the cup in Will's direction. "You ought to try thish!"

"I've tried it," Will told him. "In any case, that stuff keeps you awake and I'm feeling sleepy."

Humfrey gave him a quizzical look. "Haven't you shpent enough time shleeping?"

The Harp regarded Will with scorn as he waddled towards the door of the chamber. "Party pooper!" It turned back to the remaining companions. "OK, gang! Let's have a singsong! Is there anyone in here tonight from Dun Indewood? Well, here's one specially for you:

You put your right leg in, your right leg out,
Your right leg in and you shake it all about.
You oil it at the hinges and you turn around
And clatter and clank about.
Ohhhhh, putting on your armour..."

"You know what?" said Rose loudly. "I'm feeling pretty tired myself." She slipped through the door behind Will.

Together, they headed out of the main hall and along the marble corridors. Arriving at his sleeping chamber, Will turned to Rose. "Goodnight."

Rose gave Will a strange, almost shy look. "Yes, you are."

Will looked blank. "What?"

"You're a Good Knyght." There was a brief pause. "You are, you know. See you in the morning." With a sketchy wave of her hand, Rose turned on her heel and headed for her sleeping apartment, leaving Will staring after her wide-eyed with amazement. Slowly, an incredulous grin spread across his face as he realised that in the many months he'd known Rose, she had paid him a compliment for the very first time.

Still grinning, Will made his way into his sleeping chamber and settled himself on the vast oval bed with its cooling silk sheets and inviting plump pillows. He flung out his arms and closed his eyes, giving a grateful sigh of pleasure as an aching heaviness spread through his limbs. His breathing grew deeper and more regular as the events of the past days played out in his mind before sleep finally took hold of him.

He was surrounded by a great darkness. It was as black as the oubliette he had fallen into, but this darkness did not feel confined: it seemed infinite. A sudden wind beat at Will's face and hair. Then, from out of the darkness a figure began to form. Will gave a gasp of dismay – the Knyghtmare was back!

As quickly as it had arisen, the wind subsided. An overwhelming feeling of relief washed through Will as the Dreamwalker – vast, a deeper black against the formless darkness – materialised before him.

"Do not be alarmed," said the Dreamwalker. *"Once again I am master of my realm. You and all the sleeping creatures of the world are safe – the Knyghtmare is truly vanquished."*

Will bowed.

"Vanquished because of you," continued the creature of dreams. *"Therefore I give you thanks – Willum de Sanglier – a true Knyght: pure in heart, noble of mind."*

Will swore that he could see a faint twinkle of starlight shining in the depths of the Dreamwalker's shadowed eyes.

"In gratitude for your service, I shall reward the people of Dun Indewood. I will become their guide and protector in their sleeping hours." Seeing Will's expression, the Dreamwalker paused. *"You appear troubled by my offer."*

Will looked steadily at the Dreamwalker. *"I know I lack wisdom,"* he said carefully. *"Nor do I have your understanding of the world of dreams. But some things, I have learnt. Your offer is generous, yet I should wish that you do not seek to impose your dreams on the people of Dun Indewood."*

The Dreamwalker was taken aback. *"Explain yourself."*

"By all means offer your guidance, and direct the dreams of those who choose to accept. But I must ask that you leave those who do not choose to follow your path to dream as they will."

Deep fires glowed in the Dreamwalker's eyes. Its voice was agitated. *"But I can bring the humans of your city to* understand themselves, to face their hidden fears and secret desires – to become better people. I can help them."

"Yes," replied Will. "As long as they wish your help. Some may choose to learn from their mistakes without your advice."

"But whose dreams will they dream, if not mine?"

Will's voice was resolute. "They will dream their own dreams."

There was a deep silence. At length the Dreamwalker spoke. "I agree to your condition. I will send dreams only to those who choose to accept my guidance."

Will bowed again. "Thank you."

"We will meet again, Willum de Sanglier." There was a roar of wind and the Dreamwalker disappeared, leaving Will to sink into a slumber blessedly devoid of dreams.

Several days later, a band of travellers gathered in the outer courtyard of the Emir's palace.

Will was glad to be on the move again. After a few more Beau Reverean feasts, he wasn't sure he'd be able to get between the trees in the denser parts of the Dark Forest without turning sideways.

Rose had become quite friendly with Shayde (an alliance Will found slightly disturbing as he frequently noticed them looking in his direction with their heads together and giggling). Shayde had even prevailed upon Rose to try Beau Reverean fashions, and Will thought he detected a slightly wistful look in his friend's eyes as she smoothed down the newly cleaned and repaired (but decidedly unglamorous) tunic in which she'd arrived in the city.

The Vizier was been anxious to establish friendly relations with Dun Indewood. After some discussion, it had been decided that Shayde should act as Beau Revere's ambassador. The Vizier had argued that, as the Emir's heir, this would be valuable experience for her (and, he thought, but was careful not to say, would keep her out of trouble). Tym had initially offered to carry both Shayde and Humfrey to Dun Indewood at Whizzard speed, but Humfrey had instantly vetoed this suggestion. "No way!" the boggart had growled. "If you think I'm gonna race through the foresht on your back again, then you're one clue short of a sholution. Thish time I'm walking."

"But that will take weeks!" Tym had protested.

Staring hard at Tym, Shayde had coughed in a meaningful way.

"What am I saying?" Tym had said quickly. "Yes, that suits me fine. Weeks, possibly months..."

Humfrey eyed Tym as he helped Shayde mount the palfrey on which she was to ride, and gave Will an outrageous wink. "I forshee ructionsh when Zamarind findsh out about thoshe two lovebirdsh."

The Harp made preparatory strumming noises and cleared its throat. "I will now sing a song of farewell..."

Will thrust it to the bottom of his pack, muffling its protests by stuffing clean shirts and hose all around it. His packing completed, he bowed to Shaman and the Emir who had come to see them off.

"Rose and I will come with you some of the way," he told Humfrey. "Maybe the whole way. It's time we looked in on Dun Indewood again. Of course, we won't be staying long..."

Humfrey nodded. "Whatever you shay." He secured a sack of coffee beans on the pack mule that the Emir had provided to carry his daughter's luggage. "We'd better get shtarted. We've got a long way to go."

"Farewell," said the Vizier in a voice that was, for him, almost cordial.

"Good luck!" The Emir waved a vast silk handkerchief, then rather spoiled the effect by using it to blow his nose.

Tym and Shayde waved. Humfrey led the small procession as it moved off. Bringing up the rear, Will and Rose paused at the palace gate.

"Goodbye," called Will.

"Good fortune!" cried Rose. She grinned. "And pleasant dreams!"

I

Order Form

To order direct from the publishers, just make a list of the titles you want and fill in the form below:

Name ....

Address ....

....

....

Send to: Dept 6, HarperCollins Publishers Ltd, Westerhill Road, Bishopbriggs, Glasgow G64 2QT.

Please enclose a cheque or postal order to the value of the cover price, plus:

UK & BFPO: Add £1.00 for the first book, and 25p per copy for each additional book ordered.

Overseas and Eire: Add £2.95 service charge. Books will be sent by surface mail but quotes for airmail despatch will be given on request.

A 24-hour telephone ordering service is available to holders of Visa, MasterCard, Amex or Switch cards on 0141- 772 2281.